MYSTERY

ACTING can be MURDER

Bobbie Raymond

ALBERT'S BRIDGE BOOKS

Acting Can Be Murder

A Como Lake Players Mystery

First Edition | 2018

Albert's Bridge Books

All rights reserved. No part of this book may be used or reproduced in any manner whatsoever, including Internet usage, without written permission from the author, except in the case of brief quotations embodied in critical articles and reviews.

Copyright © 2018

This is a work of fiction. Any references to historical events, real people, or real locales are used fictitiously. Other names, characters, places, and incidents are the product of the author's imagination, and any resemblance to actual events or locales or persons, living or dead, is entirely coincidental.

ISBN-13: 978-1727536423

ISBN-10: 1727536428

Printed in the United States of America

"A dramatic critic is constantly exposed to the theater. I don't doubt some of them do develop an interest in it."

The Rev. Dr. Harper
Arsenic and Old Lace

CHAPTER ONE

"How embarrassing would it be if we got lost down here? I mean, here I am in charge of the theater and then I go and get us lost while giving a tour. Nutty, right?"

Leah turned to see how her witticism had landed, recognizing immediately that the wisecrack had fallen on the far side of flat. The young man stared back at her blankly, and on that unlined, expressionless face she read nothing but judgment. And not positive judgment. This was a decidedly negative assessment concerning her, her abilities as a tour guide and was probably inspiring a rising conviction that she was unqualified on all levels.

In short, the tour was not going well. And they were only five minutes into it.

Leah wished, not for the first time, that she had dragged Betsy along. The long-time administrative assistant had been a godsend on the last two theater tours Leah had spearheaded. And now she was questioning her decision to handle this one on her own.

However, as the recently-hired Executive Director of the Como Lake Players, Leah felt the time had come to dispense with the handholding and conduct an actual tour on her own. The interview portion with this candidate had gone fine, although she sensed that he was underwhelmed with the prospect of directing at the theater and was just going through the motions. To be fair, she was a little underwhelmed with him as well.

The appointment of a director for the last show of the season—a production of *The Importance of Being Earnest*—wasn't exactly near the top of her ever-expanding To-Do list, but it had felt like something she could knock off quickly to give herself an easy—and early–win.

This was the third interview she had conducted to fill the position. The first one had been with a cheerful, middle-aged woman named Nancy, who had a long list of children's theater credits on her resume. Leah had barely needed to ask even one question, as the woman had started talking as soon as she walked in the door, was still talking at the end of the tour, and continued chattering as Leah showed her out of the building.

While it was hard not to be impressed by Nancy's resume and enthusiasm, Leah had been unnerved by one portion of their conversation. On the subject of her rehearsal process, Nancy had casually mentioned her use of "recordings."

"I'm sorry," Leah had said as she looked up from the voluminous notes she had been taking. She had tried to capture the key points from Nancy's long-winded and rambling answers and felt she was coming up short. "Recordings?"

"For the lines," Nancy had said, as if that was all the explanation which was necessary.

"Recordings? For the lines?" Leah repeated.

Nancy nodded. "For the actors. The poor dears, they need so much help. So I record their lines for them. So they can listen to them. Over and over. And over. To get them right."

"I see," Leah said as she set her pen down. "Well, that may be necessary when working with kids, but I'm not sure our adult actors would require that. Or even permit it."

"Oh, the adult actors need it more than anyone," Nancy said with a shudder and a sigh. "If I didn't tell them how to say the lines, they would just say them any which way they like, the silly dears."

It took a moment for this to settle in. Leah blinked.

* * *

"You record line readings for certain lines in a show…?" she began, but Nancy cut her off with an agreeing nod.

"Not just some of the lines," she said emphatically. "I give them the correct reading for each and every line. All the inflections. *Every* pause. *Every* breath."

"Every breath," Leah repeated.

"It really improves the show. To hear every line, said correctly. You'd be amazed."

"I'm sure I would be," Leah said, still trying to wrap her mind around Nancy's bizarre and creativity-killing process.

She quickly completed the interview and turned the walking tour over to Betsy, following along with the older woman's practiced recitation while she tried to imagine what it would be like to provide line readings for every line in a show. As an actress, she found the idea appalling and she was glad there were other options for this position.

The interview with the second directing candidate had gone better, if only because it was less of a monologue and more of a dialog. Unfortunately, the candidate—a recent MFA graduate from a small college in Illinois—concluded every sentence she uttered with a nervous laugh, giving Leah the false impression their conversation was far funnier than it actually was.

Again, Leah completed the interview and let Betsy lead the tour through the old building, as the elderly Administrative Assistant pointed out all the nooks and crannies in the converted church which had housed the community theater for years.

The third candidate Leah interviewed—Jason, also an MFA

graduate, but from a much more prestigious school out East—had provided pitch-perfect responses to every question on her list, sounding nearly as practiced as one of Nancy's well-trained actors.

Jason had done his graduate work on Samuel Beckett ("Working from the French texts, of course!") and had plans to start his own theater company in the Twin Cities, once he found the right location. "I'd love to create interactive shows and theatrical experiences," he'd explained, "working out of a condemned building of some sort."

"Well, if you're looking for a condemned building, you've come to the right spot," Leah had said with a laugh.

Jason had merely nodded and glanced around the small Boardroom where the interview was being conducted. Like the rest of the building, the room was a bit on the drab side, dusty around the edges and in need of at least one good coat of paint.

"Let me give you a quick tour of the building," Leah said as she straightened up her papers. She stood up, signaling the interview portion was officially concluded, then opened the door to the Boardroom. She followed Jason out, turning to give the room one last look.

Yes, it could definitely benefit from, at a minimum, one coat of paint, she thought. And then she led Jason down the stairs to the lobby.

"Do you need my help on this one?"

Betsy called to her from the small work space behind the box office as Leah led Jason through the sunny lobby.

"No thanks, I think I have this one covered," Leah said with a smile and a wave, suggesting more confidence about the layout of the building than she actually possessed.

Leah understood the old church had been an ideal location for the small theater when it was originally founded. The structure was centrally located, had its own parking lot, and provided enough space on-site for not only building sets, but also storing the countless props and costumes from nearly twenty years of community theater shows.

However, even though she'd been on the job now for almost three weeks, she still got turned around in the labyrinth of rooms and cubbies in the basement. She often found herself in Prop Storage when she had intended to be in the Costume Shop. Or vice versa.

Nevertheless, she did her best to project confidence as she led Jason through the building. Although she hadn't intended to go directly to the scene shop, that's where they ended up. So she went into a short speech about how the unique layout of the building allowed them to bring large items through the overhead garage door, into the scene shop and then right onto the stage. She then steered him toward the steep stairs to the basement, the whole time extolling the virtues of the volunteers who made the theater's shows a possibility.

"It takes a village," she said as she turned left, thinking she was headed toward the Green Room and finding they were now in Furniture Storage. "The theater actually only has two paid positions: Executive Director and the Administrative Assistant. That's me and Betsy," Leah added with an unnecessary laugh.

She turned to see if Jason had joined in, but he was looking at the exposed beams in the ceiling. The look on his face suggested he wasn't entirely convinced they were providing the needed structural support. He turned and gave Leah a weak smile.

"Plus the directors," he said. "You pay the directors. Correct?"

"Well, yes," Leah agreed. "It's really just a stipend, and we keep it low enough so that it's unlikely to have any real impact on your taxes. You're welcome," she added with a forced smile.

Jason just nodded as he considered all the couches, tables, beds, chairs and desks that were piled haphazardly throughout Furniture Storage.

He turned back to Leah. "Can I see the stage?"

"Sure thing."

It took three tries, but Leah finally found the right combination of switches to turn on the lights in the auditorium and on the stage. Granted, she was only able to find power for the flat and unflattering work lights; mastering the light board in the Tech Booth was on her To-Do list, but would require some hands-on guidance from the current show's Stage Manager, a frighteningly-efficient young woman named Kanisha.

Once the lights popped on, she once again marveled at the beauty of the set. The volunteers—led by a very talented Scenic Designer who was moonlighting from his corporate gig—had created a stunning multi-level set: a late nineteenth-century Victorian-style mansion, complete with detailed flowered wallpaper, a bay window and window seat, and a sweeping staircase which led up to a row of doors on the second floor.

Although she'd had literally nothing to do with its creation, Leah looked at the set with pride, convinced it was work like this that made her decision to come back to the Twin Cities the right one. She folded her arms and smiled, turning to see if Jason was sharing in her delight at the accomplishment. Instead, the thin, pale young man was pursing his lips.

"What show is this for?" he asked, sounding only a teeny-tiny bit interested in his own question.

"We're doing *Arsenic and Old Lace*," Leah said, wondering how he had missed the oversized sign announcing that show on the theater's front lawn. "Of course, it looks even better with the stage lights on it. The volunteers we get for the lighting design here are amazing."

"Arsenic and what?" he said as he walked toward the stage.

"*Arsenic and Old Lace*," Leah repeated, saying the words more slowly in case she had raced through the title too quickly the first time.

Jason turned back, clearly not impressed with whatever he was looking at on the stage. "I'm afraid I don't know it."

"Oh. Okay," Leah said.

Jason noticed the steps at the side of the stage and gestured to them, visually requesting permission to mount the stage.

"By all means," Leah said, perhaps a bit too enthusiastically, as she followed him up to the expansive living room set. She stood center stage and watched him as he prowled the space, searching—or so it seemed—for something, anything, to capture his interest.

"I'm really surprised you've never heard of *Arsenic and Old Lace*," Leah said, trying to sound casual. "It's sort of a staple of community theaters. I even did it in Summer Stock once, back in the stone age. It's very funny and has a large cast. Plus, fortunately, only one set," she added, gesturing unnecessarily at the set around them. "All the things we look for in a good community theater show."

Jason looked over and shook his head. "Sorry, I guess I'm not as well-versed in popular theater as I should be."

"But you do know Beckett," she said.

"Him I know," he agreed.

"Well, you should check out this show sometime. Feel free to come this weekend, if you'd like. As our guest," she added quickly.

"That would be nice," Jason said. If there was a way to say it more noncommittally, Leah couldn't imagine what it might be.

Jason continued to explore all the elements of the set, while Leah did her best to not look as uncomfortable as she was beginning to feel. She paced quietly on the stage, watching him as he examined some of the minor props, taking a long moment to look at the faux grandfather clock against one wall. At one point Leah was so caught up in watching him that she nearly stepped off the front edge of the stage.

"What's sort of interesting about *Arsenic and Old Lace*," she said as she stepped back from nearly tumbling into the first row, "is that it started out as a drama and was later turned into a comedy. Same story, same set-up, but all it took were a few alterations to make it into a farce."

"Comedy's funny that way," Jason said, for some reason now closely examining the construction of the mantelpiece over the fireplace. "Beckett said in *Endgame*, 'Nothing is funnier than unhappiness.'"

"It's a wonder he wasn't invited to more parties."

Jason looked up from his inspection. "What's that?"

"Nothing," Leah said with a quick shake of her head.

Jason looked out at the empty rows of seats in the house and then once more took in the set around them. "So what's the theme?"

"Theme?"

"You know, what facet of the human condition does this play explore?"

This question brought Leah up short and so she took a moment to consider it. "Well, there's a lot of death in the play," she finally said. "It's not exactly *Hamlet*, but there are a couple bodies on stage before the final curtain."

"The critics love that," Jason said. Leah couldn't tell if he was being sarcastic or insightful.

"Well, some critics do," she said. "I wish the same could be said of our local reviewer."

"A harsh critique?"

"Brutal. The headline was something like, '*Arsenic is Dead On Arrival.*' It was all downhill from there," Leah said.

"A hatchet job?"

"Yes, quite literally as it turns out. The critic's name is Ronald Hatchet."

Jason laughed. "Looks like that poor lad's career path was set at an early age."

"Just our luck. And I thought the critics in New York could be harsh. They have nothing on Ronald Hatchet. Which is a shame," she said, "because the cast is great and they're funny and committed and the audience loves the show."

"Ah yes, the final arbiter. The dreaded general public," Jason said as he moved upstage to check out the doors, first the one to the cellar and then the one to the off-stage kitchen. Leah watched him, unsure of what the next best step might be. She took another quick look over her shoulder, to make sure she was a sufficient distance from the edge of the stage. Falling off was one way to get out of this interview, but she thought she'd consider other options first.

"Well, we're looking at several candidates, so unless you

have any other questions for me..." she said, letting her words trail off.

"'All life long, the same questions, the same answers,'" he said as he moved over to the window seat.

Leah took a stab. "Beckett?"

Jason smiled, pleased with her alleged depth of knowledge. "Indeed. *Endgame* once again." He pulled back the curtains, looked out the window and then absently opened the window seat.

"Yes, well," Leah said as she glanced at the nonexistent watch on her wrist. "Anyway ..."

She started to head back to the stairs that would take them off the stage and, with any luck, bring an end to this interview.

"One quick question," Jason said.

Leah turned back. He was standing over the open window seat, holding the lid with one hand. "Who constructs your props? This is fantastic."

Leah moved toward him, completely unsure of what he was talking about.

"We built one of these when we did Joe Orton's *Loot* back in prep school," he continued, "because of course you have to use a dummy for that show. But it didn't have near the detail of this one. Which was, I think, Orton's point. As I remember."

Whatever was in the wooden box, it was by far the most impressive thing Jason had seen since coming into the building.

Leah crossed the stage and looked into the window seat. What she saw in the box was so out of context to what she had expected, it took her several long seconds to understand what she was looking at.

And when she finally did, she couldn't help but let out a yelp.

The sound was so sudden and sharp, it startled Jason, who let go of the box's lid, letting it slam shut. He looked at Leah, who had gone white.

With a trembling hand, Leah reached down and clasped the edge of the lid, slowly re-opening the window seat. She was hoping against hope that what she thought she had seen had been some sort of optical illusion.

But it hadn't been. Leah looked into the box for a long moment as she felt her mouth go dry.

"It's the critic. Ronald Hatchet," she said, her voice coming out in a rasp. "And he's dead."

CHAPTER TWO

"I don't know why I'm crying. He really was a truly horrible, horrible person."

Detective Albertson nodded sympathetically. He gently nudged a nearby tissue box toward the weepy woman and then snuck a quick glance at his watch. This interview was going on way too long, particularly if you took into account the amount of valuable information it was uncovering. For the record, currently that amount was very small.

"So, to conclude, Miss Samuels, my understanding is that your interactions with the deceased were primarily limited to those occasions when he approached the theater's box office to pick up his show tickets? Is that correct?"

Betsy snatched one of the tissues from the box, then quickly and loudly blew her nose as she nodded at the detective's concise recap of her rambling and digression-rich testimony.

"Yes, he'd pick up his tickets from me. At the box office. And let me tell you, there was many a time I thought about really giving that odious little man a piece of my mind. Did I tell you some of the terrible things he has written about this theater and our shows?"

"You did indeed," Detective Albertson said, involuntarily holding up a hand to fend off any more of the dead critic's quotes the teary Administrative Assistant had provided. He had already filled two pages of his notebook with quickly scribbled transcriptions of the savage mini-reviews gleaned from the furious and apparently photographic memory of Betsy Samuels.

He guessed her age to be pushing this side of eighty, but there was nothing dulled about the old woman's memory. He glanced down at the quotes in front of him:

> "The Como Lake Players' production is called 'Can-Can,' but my conclusion is that, in reality, the poor, talent-starved dears 'Can't-Can't.'"

> "Is there someone in your life whom you really, really hate? If so, take my advice and send them two tickets to the Como Lake Players current production of 'Room Service,' which you will find is a dish that is being served as cold as the best revenge."

> "Kaufman and Hart titled their classic play, 'You Can't Take It With You,' but this ill-considered production should more aptly be re-named 'You Can't Hardly Watch It.'"

> "'Rosencrantz and Guildenstern Are Dead.' Ten minutes into this frenzied bit of theatrical folly gone wrong and I was praying for the same fate for myself."

This last quote jumped out from the others to Detective Albertson, as it appeared as if the acerbic critic might have finally gotten his wish.

"But other than handing him his tickets, you never had any other encounters with Mr. Hatchet?"

Betsy shook her head and reached for another tissue.

"Mercifully, no. Not since he became a critic."

"And, just to recap," Albertson continued, "when I asked who you thought might have wanted to kill him, you said 'Every blessed person who ever met the detestable little creep.' I'm just wondering: Would it be possible for you to narrow that down at all?"

Betsy considered this for a long moment. Finally, she looked up at the detective. "If his mother is still alive, you could take her off the list," she said. "But I'd keep her as an alternate."

* * *

"Your Miss Samuels did a fine job of providing background information on Mr. Hatchet's relationship with the theater," Detective Albertson said as he began his interview with Leah. "And I have the notes from your earlier conversation with Detective Dietz. So there's not much need for us to delve further into that. Unless you feel you have something of relevance to add?"

Leah was surprised to be back in the theater's small Boardroom so soon. She looked across the long oak table at the young police detective and shook her head. "I've never had any encounters with the man," she said. "This is only my third week on the job. I just moved back here."

While he made note of this, Leah made her own mental notes about him. Probably about thirty, she figured. Handsome in an average but appealing way. He clearly didn't fuss with special hair conditioners, but he knew how to buy (and wear) a good suit. And he had soft, gray eyes that seemed kind.

Detective Albertson looked up from his notes and she gave the eyes another assessment. Let's call them gray-green.

"The new kid on the block, huh?" he said with a smile.

Leah nodded. "I guess that's the case."

"Me too. Anyway, according to what you said that you told Detective Dietz, you had no idea Mr. Hatchet was in the building or any idea how his corpse came to be placed in the window seat. Is that correct?"

"Absolutely. I was giving a tour to a directing candidate and he happened to open the window seat while we were touring the set. If he hadn't done that, the body probably wouldn't have been discovered until this weekend."

"This weekend?"

"Yes, we do shows on Friday and Saturday nights, and then a Sunday matinee," Leah said. "So, in theory, the body would not have been discovered until our Stage Manager set the prop dummy we use into the window seat before the show."

"What brought you to the Twin Cities?"

This sudden shift in topic threw Leah for a moment.

"Um," she said as she tried to land on a reasonable entry point to the story that wouldn't dredge up unnecessary details. "I was living in New York, have been for many years, and decided to make a change and move back here."

"You've lived here before?"

"In college. I went to the University of Minnesota."

"Theater major?"

"Guilty as charged," Leah said and then instantly regretted the word choice. "Actually, a BFA."

"What did you do in New York?"

"I was an actress. And ran a small theater company," she said, and then added, "Co-ran it, actually."

"Good training for this job, I would imagine," Albertson said as he made more notes.

Leah nodded, wishing they could move back to talking about dead bodies. "Yes, I think that's why the Board thought I was a good choice for the job. There's an art to running a non-profit theater without running it into the ground."

"Unmarried?"

"Excuse me?"

"You're not currently married."

"Never have been," Leah said as she shook her head slowly. "How would you know that?"

"No ring on your finger," he replied, pointing his pen in the direction of her left hand.

"You don't have one either," Leah said as she pointed at his left hand. "Of course, people don't always wear them."

"No, they don't," Albertson agreed.

They locked eyes for just a few seconds longer than might have been necessary.

"My mistake," he said. "So when was the last time someone might have looked into that window seat?"

This U-turn back to questions about the murder surprised Leah. For a moment she thought this might be some sort of police interrogation technique: Keep the subject off-guard throughout the interview, which then might elicit more candid answers.

"Well, officially that would have been during the Sunday matinee," she said. "When do you think it happened? I mean, when was he murdered?"

Albertson shook his head. "We'll have to wait for a determination from the coroner to narrow it down," he said. "But based on the amount of rigor I observed, I'd say it's been at least a couple days. This is Wednesday ... so it could have happened on Sunday or Monday, but likely not later than that."

"That's a wacky observational skill you have there," Leah said, trying to bring some levity to the conversation. "Guessing the time of death based on rigor. Must be fun at parties."

He narrowed his eyes at her. "It comes in handy more often than you might imagine," he said. She couldn't quite tell if he was kidding or not.

"What about access?" he continued.

"Excuse me?"

"Who had access to the theater after hours?"

Leah considered this new line of questioning. "Quite a number of people, actually."

"Can you narrow that down?"

"Well," she said as she sorted the organizational chart out in her mind. "We're a volunteer organization and many of our volunteers come and go at odd hours. So lots of people have keys."

Detective Albertson was poised with his pen and pad. "Can you elaborate?"

"Well, the actors, of course," she began. "Designers, stage

managers, board operators. The Board Members. House Managers," she continued, not entirely sure she had hit everyone on the list. "Then, at the conclusion of a production, all the volunteers are asked to turn in their keys."

"Of course, anyone could have made a copy of their key," Detective Albertson suggested.

"Well, they do say "Do Not Copy" right on them," Leah said, "but I guess there's always going to be someone out there who finds a way to circumvent that."

"There always is."

"So what happens now?"

Detective Albertson scanned his notes one last time before he shut his notebook. "We'll do an autopsy to determine cause and approximate time of death and then investigate the last few days of Mr. Hatchet's life. See who may have had a good reason to harm him."

"Well, if you check his most recently published reviews, there are a score of actors who are happy to see him gone."

Albertson flipped opened his notebook again. "How do you figure?"

"His review of our show came out Sunday morning; he saw it on Friday night. He had another review that came out that same morning as well. It was the show he saw on Saturday night. A production of *Into the Woods*. I think the headline was something like, 'Whatever You Do, Don't Go *Into the Woods*.' If you thought he hated our show, you should read that review."

"He didn't review your show favorably?"

Leah shook her head. "I've looked through the scrapbook. He hardly ever reviewed anything this theater did favorably," she said with a laugh. "The review he gave our *Arsenic and Old Lace* was no meaner than usual, although he did single out one or two actors for some cutting remarks and also generally trashed the director."

"Did you ever confront him on the persistent negative nature of his reviews?"

Leah shook her head. "Like I said, I've only been here a few weeks."

"That's right," Albertson said. "Of course."

"But I do remember him from back when I was here in college—he was always mean-spirited, even then. One of those people who never had anything nice to say about anything or anyone."

"My mother warned me about those kinds of people," Albertson said, closing his notebook again.

"I'll just bet she did," Leah said as she began to stand up and then checked to make sure Albertson was doing the same.

"Well, Miss Sexton, if we have any further—" he began as he also stood up, but she cut him off.

"You can call me Leah," she said.

"And you can call me Mark. And you can call me any time," he added as he put out his hand. Leah went to shake it and then saw he was handing her a business card. She blushed as she took it.

"Thanks," she said as she took the card and then held it awkwardly, not sure of what to do with it. Did the slacks she'd put on this morning have pockets? For the life of her, she couldn't remember.

"I mean, call me if you think of anything else," he added.

"Sure thing, I knew that," Leah said as she turned to open the door for him.

"I'll find my way out," he said as he stepped through the doorway and into the hall.

"Absolutely, good to talk to you, thanks for stopping by," she said, and then realized she had slipped back into interview mode. "I mean, um, thank you." She watched as he headed down the hall and suddenly a thought occurred to her.

"Detective Albertson," she yelled to him a bit too loudly. He stopped and turned.

"Yes?"

"I forgot to ask the other policeman, Detective Dietz. Are we okay to use the stage this weekend? For our show? Or will it," she said, searching for the right term. "Or will it still be an official crime scene?"

He cut the distance between them by half and she did the same, placing them closer together. But not too close. He looked down at his watch.

"Oh, you should be fine. Your next show is on Friday night, right?"

"Yes. I mean, we do a speed-through on Thursday night, but we don't have to do that on-stage. The cast can do that in the Green Room."

"A speed-through?"

"Oh, right, I forgot, you're a civilian," Leah said with a laugh. "When you only do a show on weekends, sometimes a cast will get together before the Friday show to quickly run lines. You know, to refresh their memories. Sometimes they just come in early before the Friday show, but this cast elected to do their speed-throughs on Thursday nights."

Detective Mark Albertson nodded patiently throughout Leah's explanation. She hoped it hadn't seemed as long to him as it had to her while she was saying it. She felt like she'd spent the entire interview babbling ceaselessly.

"Good to know," he said. "I don't see any reason why the team won't be done with the stage later today or early tomorrow. And so I'm assuming you aren't planning to cancel shows this weekend? I mean, because of the death and the body and all?"

Leah shook her head. "We didn't even have time to consider it," she said. "Once word got out, the phone's been ringing off the hook. We're sold out for Friday and nearly sold out for Saturday night as well. And the Sunday matinee is packed."

"You have a morbid audience," he said, suppressing a grin.

"I don't doubt that's true," Leah said. "But I think these ticket buyers are a pretty even mix of accident gawkers and people who really didn't like the guy. At least, that's Betsy's assessment so far."

"Interesting," Albertson said. "So while Hatchet's review

might have hurt the show, his death is having the exact opposite effect at the box office."

"Does that constitute a motive for murder?" Leah asked as the implications of what he had said began to settle in on her.

"I'm not sure," the detective said as he turned to make his second attempt at an exit. "But it's certainly not the worst motive for murder I've ever heard."

CHAPTER THREE

"As I understand it, the key component of a speed-through is supposed to be *speed*," Alex said. "I mean, it even has the word speed in its name, for god's sake."

He threw his backpack up onto the stage and then hoisted himself onto the platform. "I'm begging you. Can't you make that woman go any faster? I swear, the last speed-through I did with her took longer than the actual play."

"Good evening, Alex. You get points for being here first," Kanisha replied as she glanced up from her seat in the front row. Her large Stage Manager's binder lay spread out on her lap. She paged through the notebook until she found the cast list she had been looking for. "Now as to your concerns about your co-actor, remember that the purpose of a brush-up rehearsal, such as a speed-through, is to provide each of the actors with the resources they need to execute their performance. Different actors have different processes."

"What, is that a quote from the *Stage Manager's Bible*?" Alex said as he dug into his backpack, searching for the apple he was sure he had tossed in there. He played Dr. Einstein in the play and as usual was virtually unrecognizable to Kanisha without his big, gray frizzy wig and walrus mustache.

"There's no such thing," Kanisha said, not looking up from her binder. "But it's not a bad idea. I should probably write one."

Alex had a snarky response locked and loaded, but then other actors began to wander onto the stage, so he set it aside for later.

Kanisha looked up at the new arrivals and then started checking off names on her cast list. *Arsenic and Old Lace* had a large cast—thirteen people—and Kanisha felt she spent way too much of her time checking to make sure everyone was present.

She noted each cast member when they appeared, while at the same time she recognized they were all actively avoiding sitting on the window seat, which was usually a popular location for the speed-through.

The last person to appear was the actress who Alex had been railing about—Joan O'Malley, who played the pivotal role of Aunt Abby in the play.

In Kanisha's view, Joan had been a royal pain ever since the audition process, when she had insisted on reading for the role of the ingénue, Elaine. The director had acquiesced, asked her to Call Backs, and then offered the middle-aged woman the more age-appropriate role of Aunt Abby.

The director had told Kanisha that when he made the phone call to offer the role, Joan audibly gasped at the suggestion. It took copious coaxing for her to accept the part, which just fueled her already massive ego. She had been impossible from that day forward.

Once Kanisha was sure everyone was present, she sent a quick text to Leah, who had said she wanted to talk to the cast before they got started.

"Good evening, everyone," Kanisha said from her front row seat. "Before we dive into the speed-through, we have a couple quick notes from last Sunday's matinee." She glanced down at her Show Report from the previous weekend.

"Everyone needs to remember to place their props back on the designated spot on the prop tables after the show; we found a couple key props still on stage during the matinee cleanup, including someone's nightstick–Officer Brophy, I'm looking at you."

"My bad," a young actor said with a grin and then returned to whatever game he was playing on his phone.

"And please remember, people," she said, raising her voice to indicate that the chattering should stop. "The food in the refrigerator backstage is *prop* food, not cast food. So hands off!"

With that declaration completed, she continued to scan the list, looking for other notes which specifically applied to the actors. There was a note on the cleaning schedule for the costume person, a mention of a burned-out light fixture for the tech director, and a repeated note for the props guy about a recalcitrant doorbell. Toward the bottom of the report, she spotted another note for the actors.

"I've reminded you of this before, but apparently it's not getting through. Do not use either of the lobby restrooms during the show. We can hear every flush clearly in the house. I know it's like a Turkish prison down there, but if you have to relieve yourself during the show, use the restroom right outside the Green Room."

"I refuse to use that restroom until it undergoes some serious scrubbing," Joan O'Malley said. "It is disgusting."

"I will make another note for the cleaning crew," Kanisha said as she dutifully added this request to her To-Do list.

"In fact, the entire Green Room could benefit from a bacterial scouring," Joan O'Malley added. "And I'm not so sure there isn't mold in the walls."

"I thought the same thing when I first saw it," Leah said loudly to the group as she made her way down the main aisle. "But I'm happy to report the Building Inspector I hired gave us a clean bill of health, at least as it relates to mold, radon, and carbon monoxide. The bats in the attic, however, are a whole 'nother story for another day."

The mention of the bats produced an audible reaction from the group. Leah had reached the stage by this point and she waited for the hub-bub to settle down.

"I think I've introduced myself to most of you. I'm Leah Sexton, the new Executive Director of the Como Lake Players," she said. She glanced over to Kanisha to make sure this was a good time for her short speech. Kanisha nodded and Leah continued.

"By now, I'm sure you've all heard about the incident which was discovered yesterday…the unfortunate death of Ronald Hatchet and the bizarre placement of his body into the window seat on our set."

Clearly no one was surprised by this news, but the cast all still turned, as one, to look at the window seat. Alex was the only one who had opted to sit there. He was munching on an apple and he nodded at all the actors who were staring at him. And then he absently glanced down at where he was sitting.

"Oh, you mean this window seat?" he said with a playful yelp as he jumped up. He laughed, sat back on the window seat and took another big bite from his apple. Leah exchanged a quick look with Kanisha, who mouthed the word they were both thinking: Actors!

"Experience has taught me that events such as this can have a profound and sometimes surprising effect on people," Leah continued. "Either immediately after the incident, or in some cases days, weeks or even months later. To that end, we've contracted with a local firm that offers counseling for victims of trauma. I've given the contact information to Kanisha and I urge you to take advantage of it if you begin to feel any emotional reaction to what happened here this week."

"What exactly did happen here," Joan O'Malley said loudly. "There was precious little in the newspaper this week and there are rumors flying around like crazy on the Interwebs. I think a little accurate information, shared with this cast, would not be an unreasonable request. In my opinion."

Leah nodded as Joan spoke. Although she was still new to this company, Leah had immediately recognized Joan as the type of personality who seemed to thrive on making things tough for everyone around her. Every theater company had one. If they were lucky, they had only one.

"Absolutely," Leah said. "I have spoken to a couple different folks in the St. Paul Police Department and this is my understanding. At some point after Sunday's matinee, someone killed the theater critic, Ronald Hatchet, and placed his body in the window seat on our set. The police are still speculating on where the actual murder took place, but they believe the body was brought to the stage after Mr. Hatchet had died. The corpse was subsequently discovered on Wednesday."

"Did they tell you how he was killed?" Joan O'Malley asked. "I mean, that would strike me as a pertinent detail and certainly something we have every right to know. They go out of their way sometimes to keep us in the dark, that's what I think."

Leah nodded along with Joan, waiting until the older woman had apparently finished. "Yes, they are still awaiting the final autopsy report, but they said they think it was likely that he was poisoned."

"Arsenic?" Alex asked. He was still seated comfortably on the window seat. "Or is that a little too on the nose?"

"As soon as I learn more, I will pass it along to your very capable Stage Manager and she will update the cast and crew as appropriate," Leah said. "And now, if there are no further questions, I'll let you get on with your speed-through. Have great shows this weekend, everyone."

Leah gave Kanisha a quick nod and then turned and started back up the main aisle. The Stage Manager flipped pages in her binder until she came to the first page of the play.

"Act One, Scene One," she said loudly. "Lights up."

There was a pause, and then Joan O'Malley began to speak. She enunciated each word with precision, drawing out the syllables and taking large pauses at each of the commas.

"'Yes, indeed, my sister Martha and I have been talking all week about your sermon last Sunday,'" she said slowly. "'It's really wonderful, Dr. Harper—in only two short years you've taken on the spirit of Brooklyn.'"

Leah, who had reached the top of the aisle by the end of the actress's first line, turned and looked back at the performers assembled on stage.

"She understands this is a speed-through, right?" she thought to herself as she stepped out of the auditorium.

On stage, the cast settled in, recognizing they were going to be there for a while. Alex took the final bite of his apple and closed his eyes, waiting for his first cue, which was a long, long way off.

CHAPTER FOUR

"I have to admit, I'm having some serious office envy here."

"What, your office doesn't have a view of the river outside one window and the Minneapolis skyline out the other?"

Leah shook her head. "I have a lovely view of a faded brick wall out my office window. It's the apartment building next door. Plus, if I crane my neck, I can also see an air conditioning unit."

"Sounds lovely."

"That's life in a non-profit theater in a nutshell," Leah said.

"I have to admit," Gloria said as she leaned back in a high-tech chair that blended perfectly with the modern decor of the rest of her office. "I don't miss those days. Community theater has its place, don't get me wrong, but big-budget theater has so many more nice…perks."

"And Vice President, Corporate Foundation, is a title that has a nice ring to it, I have to admit," Leah said. She had settled so far into the office's plush white couch that she was concerned that—when the time came–it would take one or two people to help her get out.

She took in the view that Gloria had mentioned, and then

scanned the posters on the wall. Each one touted a theater classic while boasting the big name or names who had graced the stage for that show. The roster was an even mix of Broadway luminaries and TV stars with serious acting chops. And the posters accurately reflected the opulent–and well-funded–productions which had made this large repertory theater a well-regarded icon.

"It's weird," Gloria said, lowering her voice to a whisper, although the door to her office was closed and the white noise generators were doing their job keeping office hub-bub to a minimum. "How many other theaters have so much money that they've actually appointed someone to spend their days giving it away?"

"That's a rare thing in the theater world," Leah agreed.

"Honey, that's a rare thing in the real world," Gloria said, breaking into a wide smile. "It's so good to see you."

"Thanks, but I wouldn't be here if it weren't for you," Leah said as she returned the smile. "I'm guessing it was your good word that convinced the rest of the members on the Board at the Como Lake Players to take a chance on me."

"Take a chance my ass. We are lucky to have you," Gloria said. "The Como Lake Players is a cute little theater, but the one thing I've learned on my time on the Board is they really needed someone to bring the whole organization up-to-date. When they asked for Board members to suggest candidates, you were the first person I thought of. And as it turned out, it was an ideal time for you to make a move."

"Yes," Leah said with a sigh. "When your life implodes, that's often the universe's way of saying this is the best time to make a change."

Gloria considered this. "Have you heard from him at all?"

"Dylan?"

Gloria nodded.

Leah shook her head. "No. I blocked his number on my phone the day I left and added his email address to my spam list. So even if he has tried to reach out, I'm unavailable."

"Good for you," Gloria said. "Good riddance. Although, to be honest, Dylan was easy on the eyes."

"Don't I know it," Leah agreed ruefully. "But as easy as he was on my eyes, his own eyes had a habit of drifting. A bad habit, as it turned out."

"Actors," Gloria huffed. "They're the worst parts of most men, stuffed into an attractive package. A dangerous combination.

"But," she continued as she perked up, "Look at the bright side: that relationship gave you experience in the non-profit theater world, which landed you here, squarely on your feet."

"It did do that," Leah agreed. "However, it would have been nice to get here without going through the nightmare of walking in on my boyfriend romping naked with one of our nubile young cast members. Again."

Gloria shook her head. "Dylan, Dylan, Dylan, will he never learn?"

Leah considered this for a long moment.

"No, I don't think he ever will."

"Well," Gloria said as she stood up. "Enough of that. Do you have any objections to the Foundation buying you lunch?"

"Well, I know the Como Lake Players can't afford it, so sure, that would be great," Leah said as she began the process of extricating herself from the deeply-cushioned couch. It took a little longer than she thought it would.

Rather than leave the large, multi-stage complex, Gloria opted to treat Leah to lunch in the theater's five-star restaurant, which enjoyed a stunning view of the Mississippi river from the massive building's fourth floor.

While she picked at her nouvelle cuisine salad–with its exotic vegetables and ginger-infused dressing—Leah couldn't help think of the two sad vending machines back in the Como Lake Players' dusty kitchen. One offered a slim and often warm variety of sodas, while the other presented a collection of stale candy bars and overly-salted snack items. The comparison to what was being offered at the larger theater complex was humbling at best.

She looked over at Gloria, who had ordered a rich risotto and scallops dish, which smelled divine despite its meager serving size. It was presented elegantly on a fine china plate, a far cry from the worn and wrinkly stack of paper plates available back at her tiny theater.

And instead of the aged supply of cellophane-wrapped saltines she faced every day as she passed through the dim break room, there must have been a stone or brick oven somewhere on the premises of this first-class restaurant. Both dishes were accompanied by thin, freshly baked focaccia slices, wonderfully chewy and warm to the touch.

This lunch was a far cry from Leah's standard meal of a nearly-ripe apple and a hastily thrown together sandwich, assembled from whatever ingredients in her fridge which didn't appear to have gone bad yet.

As she picked at her salad, Leah looked over at her old college friend, who as always was perfectly coifed and outfitted in a stunning pale blue ensemble. Gloria was simply one of those people who always looked put together, whether it was a college mixer ten years ago or now as a top executive at one of the largest regional theaters west of Chicago.

"So how are you settling in at the theater?" Gloria asked between bites. "That is, besides the murder and the dead body?"

"You mean, 'Other than that, how was the play, Mrs. Lincoln?'"

"Exactly. Do you feel like the place will be a good fit?"

Leah stabbed a zucchini slice while she considered the question. "Based on what I've seen so far, I think I can do a good job taking the theater to the next level. I could have done that back in New York with our little theater. Except my co-founder kept sleeping with our actresses. I don't think I'll have that problem here."

"And you're okay putting your acting career on the back-burner?"

Leah laughed. "Lately, my acting career has been put so far back on the back-burner that you can't even see it from the stove anymore." She picked up a focaccia slice and dipped it in the olive oil on the small plate in front of her. "So, yeah, I'm okay not acting for a while and focusing on this little theater."

"I hear good things about the show."

"You missed a terrific opening night," Leah said.

"Sorry. We had a big donor event here that evening," Gloria said. "By which I mean, we had a small event, but the donors were big. However, I'm going to try to come see it this weekend. I'll give you a full report."

"Okay, but be careful what you say about it after you see it," Leah said as she finished the piece of focaccia and reached for another. "Things did not end up well for the last person who badmouthed that show."

CHAPTER FIVE

As was her habit, Kanisha made a quick sweep through the Green Room after arriving at the theater. Her first priority was to post the sign-in sheet for the cast, which was her sole method of knowing when all the actors had shown up and were on the premises. But she also used the time to check the Green Room and adjoining make-up area to make sure it was free of props that should rightfully be upstairs on the props table.

As she ripped down last Sunday's sign-in sheet and replaced it with the one for this evening's show, she was surprised to see that someone had tacked up a copy of Ronald Hatchet's review of the show. It was an unwritten rule that only truly positive reviews were ever posted and, in her mind, this one fell far from that standard. While it praised the dreaded Joan O'Malley, it also included some really cutting remarks about Alex's interpretation of Dr. Einstein, it slammed Doris Pepper's portrayal of Aunt Martha, and it mocked the sexual chemistry between the two actors playing the romantic leads.

This last bit was particularly ironic, Kanisha thought, as those two young actors had not been able to keep their hands off each other since the first day of rehearsal. It struck her as a classic show romance, which would burn hot and bright for the duration of the show and then flame out into a tiny ember after strike.

Kanisha read through the review again, surprised at how mean-spirited it was. There were times she agreed with critics on the shows she stage-managed—even, on rare occasions, agreeing with Hatchet himself—but in this instance, the review felt really off the mark. She found Alex to be hysterical (although would never let him know it) and believed that Doris' portrayal of Aunt Martha was really, really strong. So strong, in fact, that she had felt from the beginning that the actresses playing the two Aunt's should have switched roles, with Doris playing the more important role of Aunt Abby.

This was just one of the countless examples of a director who had followed their own flawed vision rather than having the wisdom to take Kanisha's casting advice. When would they ever learn, she thought as she gave the Green Room one last look and then headed up to prep the stage for that night's show.

* * *

Alex wasn't what you would call a 'method actor,' at least as far as he understood the term. He'd read an interview with Laurence Olivier years ago, in which the famed actor had said that he often discovered the secret to a role only once he had found the right pair of shoes or the correct mustache. While he wasn't putting himself in the same category as that classic British actor, Alex often felt the same way about how he approached a character.

That was certainly true of how he came to inhabit Dr. Einstein in *Arsenic and Old Lace*. On the page, the character had appeared merely drunken and a bit whiny. But once he had slipped on the wild gray wig and droopy white mustache, Alex felt the character come to life within him.

It had been the director's idea for the literal interpretation of Dr. Einstein, suggesting the hair and makeup that would allow him to resemble the renowned physicist. Alex wasn't sure if this had been to immediately establish the character's comic potential for the audience ... or if the director simply didn't get the joke of the name and thought the character really was Albert Einstein.

At this point, it didn't matter to Alex. He was thrilled with the comic bits he'd discovered in rehearsal and the response he'd been getting from the audience. He recognized that a lot of the credit went to the gangly actor who played the menacing Jonathan Brewster. He did a great slow burn and provided the reactions to Alex's antics that were inspiring some of the biggest laughs in the show.

Alex looked up from applying his makeup, glancing over at the bulletin board across the room. He wondered who had posted the Hatchet review and for a moment he began to stew again about some of the things the dead critic had written about him, most of which he could recite from memory:

"On the weaker side of the comic ledger we find Alex Knox, whose mugging, tone-deaf performance as the ineptly murderous Dr. Einstein fails to find the laughs it so desperately seeks. A firm and consistent directorial hand might have reined him in, but it would take a miracle to make him funny."

There were some actors who never read reviews until after a show closed. After reading that one, Alex decided that was the kind of actor he should become.

* * *

Doris wasn't thrilled to be sharing a makeup mirror and tabletop space with Joan O'Malley and if there had been any other options, she would have taken them. However, by the time she had brought her things to the dressing room for the first full-dress rehearsal two weeks before, all the other spots had been taken.

She wasn't sure if the rest of the cast were consciously

avoiding Joan, but she would not have blamed them if they had. The woman had, at one time or another, annoyed or alienated just about every member of the cast. Doris herself had been on the receiving end of Joan's ire from the first rehearsal; in fact, from the first line she uttered.

"You're not going to say it like that, are you?" Joan O'Malley had barked. "You're going to need to give me more than that, in order for my lines to make sense."

That brief exchange had pretty much set the tone for the whole rehearsal process: The other actors were either too loud or too quiet, too slow to pick up a cue or too quick to respond, thus cutting into Joan's laugh line. She had actually said to Monica, the young actress playing the ingénue, "If you ever move again while I'm saying something funny, I promise you they will find your lifeless body under the stage at the end of the show."

Doris tried to reassure the young actress not to take it personally, but nevertheless the poor girl now always stood stock still on stage any time Joan was honking out one of her lines. Assuming, of course, that Joan had remembered to utter the line in the first place. She missed or mis-spoke lines so often that Doris often found herself uttering her own lines and then those of the actress playing her sister, in an ongoing attempt to keep the play and the plot moving forward.

"Good evening," Doris said as Joan settled loudly into the chair next to her at the makeup table. "They say it's a full house tonight."

"That just means more coughing and wheezing as far as I'm concerned," Joan said as she thrust her large bag onto the table with a heavy thud. "Some nights, it's like a hospital ward out there."

Before Doris could comment on the inevitability of cold and flu season, Joan was already onto another topic.

"And could there be more potholes in that minefield they laughingly call our parking lot? I swear the suspension on my Prius will be shot by the end of this run. I should send them a bill is what I should do."

Doris made sounds of approval, hoping that would be enough to nip this conversation in the bud. But instead, for some reason, Joan leaned in close and brought her voice down to the lowest level Doris had ever heard. Although it was quiet, it was not nearly a true whisper.

"I can't believe someone posted that review," Joan said in her faulty murmur.

Perhaps her ability to whisper doesn't work well due to lack of use, Doris thought. But before she could even smile at her small, internal joke, Joan continued.

"How embarrassing," Joan hissed as she glanced over at the bulletin board. "While I'm always pleased to receive a positive notice, it seems so tacky to hang it up here when so many others in the cast weren't singled out for the level of praise I received. And so many were criticized so harshly."

As one of the others who had been criticized harshly—Ronald Hatchet had said of her: *"Doris Peppers' work pales in comparison with the high-wattage of Joan O'Malley's illuminating performance"*—Doris agreed that it would have been more thoughtful to not have posted the review in the first place.

"Yes," Doris agreed quietly. "Sometimes people just don't think these things through—"

She was cut off from finishing her comment as Joan turned and barked at Kanisha, who was moving through the room.

"That doorbell," Joan said as she turned to the passing Stage Manager. "Please tell me that the dreaded doorbell has been repaired, tested and is one hundred-percent foolproof? I refuse to be left adrift on-stage awaiting a cue that refuses to make itself heard."

Kanisha stopped and smiled down at the older actress. This was the beginning of yet another pre-show diatribe from the annoying woman and she was determined to provide a professional response, regardless of how much she would rather read Joan the riot act. Nothing was ever right with this one, but the beleaguered stage manager had resolved not to sink down to her level but instead to take the high road.

Kanisha took a deep breath, working hard to keep her tone civil. "We have repaired the bell and tested it several times, with positive results every single time. Plus, I've informed the other actors that—in the unlikely event the bell refuses to work–they should simply knock on the door. As one would do."

"Knock on the door? Well, that could throw me off if I'm expecting the cue to be a doorbell and I hear a knock instead," Joan said, turning to Doris for support on this key issue. "Don't you agree that would be off-putting?"

"I can work with a bell or a knock," Doris said quickly, abandoning her makeup and getting up to pull her costume off the rack. "And if all else fails, they can always just yell, 'Is anyone home?'"

"Well you are to be commended," Joan said, although her tone did not sound particularly complimentary. "I'm afraid I can't just 'wing it' like that, not at this stage of the game. That's not how we did it in Pittsburgh."

That phrase—"That's not how we did it in Pittsburgh"–was a frequent refrain for Joan, an ongoing reminder to one and all that she had in fact attended The School of Drama at Carnegie Mellon. She used the phrase so often throughout rehearsal that Alex had considered having it printed up on t-shirts for the rest of the cast. However, when he priced out the joke, he decided it wasn't worth the expense. Instead, he modified the phrase and could often be heard muttering, "That's not how we did it in Brainerd."

Joan O'Malley returned to opening her makeup kit, turning her back on the Stage Manager, signaling—with her body language—that the conversation had concluded as far as she was concerned.

Kanisha looked at her for a long moment and then yelled to the rest of the room.

"Thirty-minutes, people!"

This produced a chorus of the traditional "Thank you, thirty," from the cast. Kanisha made her way out of the Green Room, glad to have the conversation with that dreaded woman behind her.

* * *

"I just love the way you say 'Thank you, thirty,'" Monica said quietly to Lucas, who sat next to her at the makeup table they shared. Lucas was just putting some final touches on his hair. Lucas spent an inordinate amount of time on his hair before a show, subduing each wisp and lock until he was satisfied with the arrangement.

"It's a sign of respect, which is an integral part of the relationship between the actor and the stage manager," Lucas said. He seemed finally content with the way his hair had settled after his last brushing was completed. "Too many actors don't honor the relationship, but I think theater is made by every person on the team. Not just the actors on stage."

"That's so true," Monica agreed as she applied her first layer of eye shadow. This was the base, the light blue layer. Darker shades would be coming in subsequent passes.

Monica spent much of her time agreeing with Lucas, although if pressed she would likely admit that she didn't always fully understand what he was saying. This was her first community theater show after college, while Lucas had already done at least a half-dozen shows, three of them with the Como Lake Players. So she took his word as gospel.

When she was first cast as Elaine, Monica had immediately tracked down the movie version of *Arsenic and Old Lace*. Once she was able to get over the fact the whole thing was in black and white, she had really enjoyed it, particularly watching her character interact with Cary Grant. When she told Lucas she had watched the movie version, he had clucked his tongue and said that he never looked at anything but the primary text. "For me," he had said gravely, "it's all about my liaison with the text."

Monica didn't really understand what that meant, but she made a mental note not to mention that she had watched the movie a couple more times, because she loved watching Cary Grant.

"How are you going to feel tonight when you open the window seat?" she asked, moving to the next layer of eye shadow. "I mean, now that there actually was a dead body in there earlier this week."

"There has always been a dead body in the window seat," Lucas said seriously as he touched up the hint of pink he had applied to each of his cheeks.

"What do you mean?" Monica was concerned there had been other murders in the theater besides the one with the critic and that she was just now hearing about it.

"I mean every time I—as Mortimer—open the window seat at that point in the timeline, I see a dead body. Because there is a dead body in there. Because my aunt has murdered a man and placed his body in the window seat."

Monica was feeling a bit lost. "But there isn't really a body in the window seat, right?" she asked slowly. "Just that dummy they made up. Right?"

He patted her hand and spoke more slowly. "It isn't me looking in the window seat, hon. It's Mortimer looking in the window seat. And Mortimer sees a dead body and that's how I play it. So whether there's a body in there or not makes no difference, because Mortimer sees a body and I am Mortimer. Understand?"

Monica did not understand, but she nodded as if she did, in the hope that they could change the topic to something less confusing. Like where they might go out to eat after the show.

She hoped they could get nachos and so she turned to thoughts of what variety she might order. Lucas had his own pre-show ritual and this was hers—figuring out what to eat after the show.

Monica glanced at Lucas, who had begun his pre-show humming, which he said was a form of vocal warmup. To her it just sounded like humming, but he had explained to her once–at great length–about how each note warmed up a different segment of his vocal chords, which he called his "instrument."

Monica hadn't understood it then and she didn't understand it now. Instead, she turned her attention back to her eye makeup, while in her mind she ran through a rich and inviting menu of nacho options she might enjoy after the show.

CHAPTER SIX

Leah had made a point of seeing every performance of the play since she'd arrived. So she was pretty sure it wasn't just her imagination that there was a special buzz running through the audience at this evening's show. It had been there from the beginning, but it reached its peak just before the character of Mortimer opened the window seat for the first time and discovered his murderous Aunts' handiwork.

The audience–most of whom clearly knew about the recent death of Ronald Hatchet and the unique location where his body had been found–tittered each time Mortimer Brewster got close to the window seat. Their sense of anticipation was palpable and although none of the actions on stage had changed for this performance, they all seemed to take on a new meaning based on the recent murder.

In the few times she'd seen the show, Leah had always felt the young actor playing Mortimer—she thought his name might be Lucas—tended to seriously underplay this moment and he was true to form this evening. However, his first line after seeing the body (*"Aunt Abby! You were going to make plans for Teddy to go to that ... sanitarium—Happy Dale?"*) got a bigger laugh than usual. Unless she was just imagining it. His line reading had been, to her ear, the same. So it must have been the audience's special knowledge–that the critic who trashed the show and then found himself dead on its set–was making the reaction funnier from beyond the grave.

The whole first act had this special feeling of electricity to it, right through the entrance of the homicidal Jonathan Brewster and the drunken Dr. Einstein—once again played brilliantly by an actor whose name she kept forgetting. She'd thought Ronald Hatchet's review had been way off base in several areas and the key one was slamming the performance of the actor playing Dr. Einstein. He got huge laughs by throwing away simple lines *("I was intoxicated.")*, while his lanky scene partner did a great job of understating his murderous reactions.

The first act curtain produced such thunderous and sustained applause that, for a brief moment, Leah thought they should try to figure out a way to discover the corpse of a local critic on stage every week. However, she rejected the idea immediately, as she knew there weren't enough theater critics in the area to make this work on a consistent basis. So she headed to the lobby to see where she could lend a hand.

After checking in with the volunteers operating the concession stand–to make sure they weren't running out of any of the high-volume and highly-profitable items—Leah added more season ticket brochures to the stack by the front door. She then swung by the box office, where Betsy was just finishing tallying up the night's receipts.

"That was a solid sell-out, dear" the older woman said with a touch of glee. "Have not seen one of those in a long time. Not since we had that naked Adonis prancing around in *Equus*. And, income-wise, tomorrow night looks to be more of the same."

"Excellent," Leah said, holding her hand up for a high-five. But Betsy was already onto her next task, so Leah sheepishly lowered her hand and headed back to the concession stand to see if they needed any additional assistance before the intermission came to an end.

The size of the crowd in the small lobby hindered swift

movement on her part and despite her best efforts, she jostled one of the patrons as she pushed her way through the throng.

"Excuse me," she said and then realized she knew the man she had just bumped. "Oh, Detective Albertson. You came to the show, how nice."

He smiled down at her, a plastic cup of wine in his hand. "Well, you made a strong case for it and I was free tonight," he said with a smile.

"Had I known you were coming, I would have gotten you a comp," she said. "You were lucky to get a ticket—we're sold out."

"I see that, congratulations. You seem to have a hit on your hands."

"Apparently," she agreed, turning so she could actually face him. "I think the publicity boost we got this week helped at the box office."

Mark Albertson looked around the crowded lobby. "So it would seem," he said. "I'm guessing this is a larger crowd than usual?"

"Oh my, yes," she said. "If we hit sixty-percent capacity, we're having a really outstanding night. Sell-outs are rare but much appreciated."

"Was that one of your mandates when they hired you?" he asked with a smile. "Create more sell-outs?"

Leah was thrown by the word 'mandate,' and it took her several seconds to realize he wasn't talking about a date with a man, which was where her subconscious had led her. Before she could respond, the lobby lights flickered on and off quickly, signaling the end of the intermission.

Leah glanced at her watch and did some quick math in her head—Kanisha, the Stage Manager was right on time and running a tight ship. Leah turned back to Detective Albertson and struggled for something clever to say. But the best she could come up with was, "Enjoy the second act."

"Thanks, I'm sure I will." He turned to head back to the auditorium, but Leah tapped him on the shoulder before he could get very far.

"Sorry, Detective Albertson," she said, really wishing she could leave him with a different thought.

"Mark," he said with a grin.

"Mark," she continued, "I'm sorry, but you can't take that cup with you into the theater."

"Oh, of course." He drained the rest of the wine, then looked around for a receptacle. Leah held out her hand.

"I can take care of that for you," she said, taking the cup as he and the rest of the crowd make their way back to their seats.

* * *

Acts Two and Three (which the show's director had artfully combined into one slightly-long unbroken act), maintained and built on the energy established in the first act. As a result, the show ended with a sustained standing ovation—and not one of those obligatory standing ovations, but a heartfelt expression from a truly well-entertained audience.

The crowd was still chuckling and buzzing as they exited the theater, buoyed by the show's clever closing lines *("I thought I'd had my last glass of elderberry wine." "No, here it is.")*. Leah stood off to the side, thanking the guests when they caught her eye and handing out season ticket brochures to anyone who expressed the slightest interest.

While she had done this at the end of every show, tonight she was hoping she had picked the correct of two exit doors, so she could casually bump into Detective Mark Albertson again. She scanned the faces of the exiting patrons.

"Miss Sexton!"

Leah recognized the voice and turned to see Claudia Moffatt, a prominent and outspoken member of the theater's Board. The few encounters Leah had had with the imposing woman had been short but intense and left her feeling a little battered.

Claudia Moffatt possessed no shortage of opinions and she was not shy about voicing them, often loudly and at great length.

"Miss Sexton," Claudia repeated, a little out of breath. "I wanted to introduce you to two of our key benefactors." She turned and gestured toward an older couple who were just exiting the auditorium. "Bea and Abe Kaufman, this is our theater's new Executive Director, Leah Sexton."

Claudia Moffatt was a large woman and she seemed to tower over the elderly couple, who both appeared to be well into their eighties. They looked from Claudia to Leah expectantly.

"It's a pleasure to meet you," Leah said, shifting the brochures to her left hand so she could reach out and shake hands with the two seniors. "Thanks so much for your support of the theater."

"We've been here since the beginning," Abe began, but Bea cut him off.

"First show, first night," Bea said. "Haven't missed a show since."

"The Kaufman's have been extremely generous," Claudia added. "Very thoughtful. Very generous." She put a spin on 'generous' the second time she said it and Leah picked up on the not so subtle hint.

"We really appreciate your support," Leah said. "We couldn't do it without patrons such as yourselves. I hope you enjoyed tonight's show."

"Wonderful–," Abe said, and again Bea cut him off.

"Delightful," Bea said and then she moved in close and lowered her voice. "Never did like that Hatchet fellow. I don't want to speak ill of the dead, but he was bad news. Never a kind word."

"Too negative," Abe agreed, nicely matching his wife's conspiratorial tone.

"But here's the thing," Bea continued. "You need to do more Shaw. The theater doesn't do enough Shaw. So many great plays to choose from."

Leah thought back to the long list of past productions that

hung in the theater's Board room. "Well, the theater just did *Saint Joan* last year, I think," she said while mentally scanning the list.

"Oh, but they cut it so. I hardly recognized it."

"We were home before eleven, which never happens with Shaw," Abe added.

"You did the same thing with *Heartbreak House* ten years ago," Bea continued. "Talk about a heartbreak! Too many cuts. Just too many."

Leah's first instinct was to point out that she had actually never cut anything from a Shaw play, as she'd never produced, directed or acted in one. But she understood she was representing the theater and its long history, which apparently this couple had experienced from day one.

"Well, we haven't locked down the next season completely," she said. "I'll pass your concerns along to the Play Selection Committee, and I'll be sure to let them know that when we're doing Shaw, we should do it uncut."

"Yes," Bea said, nodding along. "Except for *Man and Superman*. That one is interminable."

"You can't cut that one enough, if you ask me," Abe said.

"We'll keep that in mind," Leah said, employing her best reassuring tone. "Thanks again for coming tonight and for all your support."

"No, thank you dear," Bea said, patting her hand. "And remember: Think Shaw."

"Uncut," Abe added.

"Except for *Man and Superman*," Leah said.

"Bingo," Bea said with a wide smile. She and her husband moved away, heading slowly toward the exit door. Claudia watched them go.

"Thanks for that," she said as she turned toward Leah. "They are rich as Croesus and it would behoove us to keep them happy. They've put the theater in their will. So, is there actually any Shaw in next year's season?"

Leah shook her head. "Not currently, but I can always talk to the Play Selection committee and suggest it wouldn't hurt to consider it."

"I'd use a stronger word than consider, but I leave that up to you," Claudia said. "How are you settling in?"

"Besides the murder, just fine," Leah began, but Claudia cut her off.

"Oh, there are the Cunninghams—I need to say hello to them, press the flesh, you know. Where there's a will there's a way," she said with a laugh. And with that, she pushed and maneuvered through the dwindling crowd toward another aging couple.

Leah watched her go and then scanned the crowd to see if Detective Albertson was visible. He wasn't evident in the small number of audience members who were exiting the auditorium. She glanced into the lobby and didn't see him there, either.

"Damn," she whispered, and then shifted the season ticket brochures back into her right hand and looked to see if any remaining patrons might be interested in grabbing one.

CHAPTER SEVEN

"The first one in. The last one out."

Kanisha silently whispered this mantra to herself as she made one final sweep through the theater to ensure that all the cast, crew and audience members had in fact departed. Only then would she shut off all the lights—save for the ghost light on the stage—and lock up the theater for the night. This last task would conclude the long list of duties of—in this case—a very weary Stage Manager.

She'd already checked the auditorium and then the lobby restrooms, investigating each stall, on the off chance that one of the theater's older patrons had fallen asleep (or worse) on the toilet. As far as she knew, that had never happened, but given the demographics of the typical Como Lake Players audience member, it was not an inconceivable event.

Once when asked to describe representative audience members, she had quipped it consisted of "eighty-year-old women escorting their mothers." It was funny, she thought, because it was just on this side of true.

The main lobby was deserted and so she headed to the back stairs which would take her down for one final check of the dressing rooms and the Green Room. As she descended the steep stairs, she thought she heard a radio somewhere in the distance playing a mournful song. But as she moved closer, Kanisha recognized the sound as a low, steady moan. It sounded human, but there was an animal edge to it, like a wild creature in pain.

Kanisha stopped halfway down the steps and listened. Early in her career she had stumbled upon two actors *in flagrante delicto*—as her first theater professor used to call it—and it was something that, once experienced, she never needed to see again.

The lights were off in the hall at the base of the stairs, but the Green Room lights were on, casting enough illumination for her to recognize there was a shape of some kind crumpled at the bottom of the stairs.

As she got closer, she realized the moans were coming from the shape and that the shape was a body. A single body.

Lying sprawled at the bottom of the stairs.

And the sounds were not sounds of pleasure, but instead eerie moaning, like death was just moments away.

*** * ***

Jimmy's Bar was a favorite hang-out of the cast and crew for many reasons—low drink prices, large appetizer sizes and always a good music selection on the ancient jukebox. But everyone knew that the primary reason it was the favorite post-show hangout was its location. It was situated just across the street from the theater.

Due to this happy accident, the elapsed time from taking your final bow to grabbing a table and placing first orders could be as little as five minutes–depending on how much makeup you needed to remove and how many buttons you had on your costume. Some actors had been known to make the trek in less time than that.

By the time Alex made it to the bar, most of the cast members were already seated and sipping their first drinks. Clearly taking off Dr. Einstein's makeup, wig and mustache were consuming precious moments that could have been spent drinking, he realized. Such was the downside of his dedication to his craft.

It wasn't written anywhere, but the younger and older cast members tended to separate in the bar like oil and water. It wasn't vindictive or even consciously planned; actors just seemed to self-select to the table which was closest to their age range.

Alex was always a little torn on which table to choose. Since he was in his early thirties, he certainly was within his rights to head to the younger table; however, he also enjoyed his time with the older actors, who had great stories which were fun to listen to no matter how many times he'd heard them before. In the interest of fairness, he tended to split his time between the two camps pretty evenly.

Tonight as he crossed the room, he mentally tossed a coin and pulled up a chair at the younger actors' table, which had nearly reached capacity. Monica was there with Lucas, along with the actor who played Teddy and the three young actors who played the police in the show.

Due to some sort of statistical anomaly, the names of all three actors who played cops were a variation on Daniel—one Daniel, one Dan, and the lone female cop, Dannie. To avoid confusion, the show's director had opted to call each by their character name (Brophy, Rooney and O'Hara, respectively) and this habit had been adopted by the rest of the cast.

As if that name situation wasn't difficult enough, the director also had the brilliant idea to cast a guy named Eddie to play Teddy, Mortimer's insane younger brother who believes he is Teddy Roosevelt. After juggling the two names for the first few days of rehearsal, everyone ultimately just called him Teddy and was done with it.

And—since Eddie already sported Teddy's requisite walrus-like mustache—the time he needed to change after the show was far less than the transformation Alex was required to go through. Consequently, Teddy was already well into his first drink by the time Alex sat down.

"Let me guess," Alex said as he waved to the passing waitress. She nodded that she would return and he turned to the group. "You guys are either talking about an audition that's coming up, an audition you think you just nailed, or an actor who got a part—unjustly—that you auditioned for. Which one is it?"

There was a strained moment of silence at the table, followed by a burst of laughter from everyone. Except Lucas.

"You nailed it, Alex," Teddy said, turning to point at Lucas. "Luke here just auditioned for *Arcadia* out in Bloomington."

"Lucas," Lucas corrected quietly.

"Cool," Alex said. "Valentine or Septimus?"

"Either one, but they're calling me back for Septimus."

"Congrats, man," Alex said. "That's a good role."

Teddy started to ask a question, but the waitress returned and Alex placed his drink order, adding on an order of onion rings. Once that was done, Alex turned back to the group.

"Did you audition for that show too?" Teddy asked once he had Alex's attention.

"Sure. It's *Arcadia*. I'd be an idiot not to," Alex said.

"Did you get called back?" Teddy asked the question, and then turned to Lucas, then back to Alex.

"I did," Alex said. "And yes, it's for Septimus, but I'd much rather play Nightingale."

"You're too young for Nightingale," Teddy said and others at the table made sounds of agreement.

"Yeah, and I'm also too young to play Dr. Einstein, but here we are," Alex said. "I think Nightingale doesn't have to be an older guy, he just has to possess the prejudices of an older guy. However, Septimus is a great role as well."

He picked up one of the spare glasses of water in front of him and raised it toward Lucas. "*'When we have found all the mysteries and lost all the meanings, we will be all alone, on an empty shore,'*" he said, quoting from his recent memory of reading that line at the audition. "Here's to a successful call-back for one. And all," he added with a broad grin.

Lucas mirrored the gesture with his own glass, but his grin was far less convincing.

* * *

While the actors at the "older" table tended to arrive later, they also were inclined to leave sooner than their younger counterparts. They ordered fewer drinks, ate fewer greasy appetizers, and spent surprisingly little time talking about the current show, the next show, headshots, agents, auditions, or any other topics of interest to younger actors.

They'd had all those conversations over the years and now seemed to prefer chatting about the current political climate, the climate in general, and the adventures of their children and grandchildren.

Doris headed toward their table just as the actor playing Mr. Witherspoon arrived from the bar. He set his drink down and held a chair for her, perfectly in keeping with the faux British attitude he sported.

In reality, his name was Clyde Henderson and he had been raised on a farm in the quad cities region of Iowa. But you'd never know that by talking to him. His accent had that mid-Atlantic sound favored by movie actors of the late thirties and he was ridiculously well-read.

"Thank you, Clyde," Doris said with a shy smile.

"My pleasure," he said. "Delightful show this evening."

"It was fun, wasn't it?"

"There is nothing like playing to a full house." This came from Stuart Wilde, who was already seated. He played the Rev. Dr. Harper, but couldn't have been more dissimilar from the pious minister. He favored off-color jokes and suggestive limericks and always had one at the ready.

"Say, I heard this one today and couldn't help think of our dear Mr. Witherspoon," Stuart said with a grin. *"There was a young fellow named Clyde / who fell in the outhouse and died. / Along came his brother / and fell in another / and now they're interred side by side."*

This produced a burst of ruckus laughter, primarily from Stuart, but both Doris and Clyde offered polite chuckles at the poem. They exchanged a glance which expressed their diminishing interest in limericks, but both were polite enough to keep those thoughts to themselves.

"That's a good one, Stuart," Clyde said as sincerely as he could. "I don't know how you come up with all those. Week after week."

"The Internet, mostly," Stuart said, wiping a tear away with a paper napkin. "I belong to a couple of groups on Facebook. I think I have another one here..."

With that he took out his phone, along with his glasses, and began to scroll through the small screen, searching for an elusive limerick.

"Did your family make it tonight?" Doris asked, turning to Clyde.

He shook his head. "My dear wife is coming tomorrow night, the progeny on Sunday. Which reminds me, I neglected to send them my comps."

"I've only used one, if you need more," Doris said, reaching for her purse. "I think I have them here." She began to dig through the jumbled mess, but Clyde waved it away.

"No, thanks so much, but I'm good. I've got all I require. But if any of the grand-progeny decide to attend, I may hit you up for one or two."

"Not a problem," Doris said as she gave up the search and turned to see if the waitress was within sight.

"Don't hold your breath, if you're waiting for service," Clyde said. "I ended up making my own trek to the bar for a libation," he added, gesturing to the drink he'd carried over.

"Here's the other one I saw, made me think of you. You work in a bank, right?" Stuart asked as he glanced up from his phone.

"I did," Clyde said. He looked over at Doris who gave him a sympathetic look.

"There was a young seaman named Clanker / who needed a loan for a tanker. / They rejected his credit / right after they read it. / So he said, 'That old banker's a wanker.'"

This led to another burst of laughter, again only from Stuart.

However, his loud enjoyment was quickly drowned out by the sounds of approaching sirens. The wailing shrieks were accompanied moments later by flashing lights, as a police car and an ambulance screeched to a halt in front of the theater across the street.

Everyone in the bar turned to the wall of windows which faced the old church, as the red and blue lights bounced around the bar like a disco ball which had suddenly come to life.

* * *

The sound of the light rail train passing by her small condo apartment didn't bother Leah. Even when she was trying to fall asleep without success, as she was tonight, she actually found the sound to be oddly comforting. She had become accustomed to a similar sound during the years she and Dylan had shared an apartment in Brooklyn.

Those trains ran much closer to that building than it did here in St. Paul; it used to shake the windows and vibrate the cups and plates in the kitchen cabinets. Here in her new place, it consisted of a comforting rumble which often lulled her to sleep. It wasn't having that effect tonight, but she was pretty sure it wasn't the train's fault.

It had been a trying and stressful week and although going into a sold-out weekend of shows should have provided a reassuring sensation, Leah wasn't feeling it yet. She was too new to the job and that—coupled with the murder and the discovery of the body—had thrown her rhythms out of whack. And so she was paying for it now as she stared at the ceiling, watching the moving patterns of light provided by the passing train.

As was her custom, she re-ran recent conversations through her brain, always coming up with smarter, faster, funnier answers than she had been able to provide at the time.

She thought about the interview with the all-business Detective Dietz and the follow-up interview with the much-more-charming Detective Albertson.

She re-ran the encounter with the Board Member, Claudia Moffatt, and the charming old pair of donors, wondering if she'd been too ingratiating with the seniors. The Kaufmans. That was it, they were the Kaufmans.

She struggled to find a way to commit that name to memory, but then she was back to Detective Albertson. This time she was echoing their short exchange in the lobby, parsing each of his responses for hidden meanings and deeper interest. Unless she was imagining it–which wouldn't be the first time–he had been on the cautious side of flirtatious. Perhaps so cautious that it didn't even really qualify as true flirtation.

She had just started to re-run the lobby conversation for the third time when her phone rang, with that piercing ring tone she kept planning to change but still hadn't gotten around to. The shrill sound of the phone made her realize she had, if only for a moment, actually started to drift off to sleep.

She answered the phone and ten seconds into the frenzied conversation with Kanisha the Stage Manager, she found she was completely and utterly awake.

Leah was dressed and out the door less than five minutes later.

CHAPTER EIGHT

"It's Joan. Joan O'Malley. She fell down the back stairs!"

Kanisha, the usually completely-controlled Stage Manager, had spit out the words haltingly, clearly still upset by the events of the last 45 minutes.

By the time Leah arrived, the theater was lit up inside and out. An ambulance was just pulling away, its siren blaring, when she discovered Kanisha standing by the theater's front door. Police cars were parked haphazardly in front of the old church.

"Wait, wait, back up. So who was it who fell?"

"Joan O'Malley. She's the one who plays Abby Brewster," Kanisha explained.

"And that was Joan in the ambulance?" Leah said, trying to piece things together. "And you said, she fell down the stairs?"

"Yes, the stairs down to the Green Room," Kanisha repeated, taking a deep breath, trying to calm herself down. "She told me someone pushed her, but that's all I heard before she passed out. The EMTs said she has, at minimum, two broken legs and a possible concussion. She was very lucky—she could have broken her back."

Or her neck, Leah thought, but kept that idea to herself.

"Was she able to say who pushed her?" Leah asked. Kanisha continued to shake her head.

"No, the police asked the same thing. That was all she said, that someone pushed her. They said they're going to question her in the hospital, once she regains consciousness."

Kanisha produced a tissue from the inside of her sleeve and gave her nose a quick blow. "I'm so glad I made one last sweep through the building. She could have lain there all night!"

"If it was at the base of the stairs to the Green Room, it might have been well into tomorrow afternoon before we found her," Leah said as she ran the theater's Saturday schedule through her mind. There would be a show on Saturday night, of course, but nothing else was scheduled to be going on in the building during the day. She patted the young woman's back. "You did great, Kanisha."

Kanisha nodded and then blew her nose again.

Leah's attention was drawn to movement near the three squad cars at the curb. A new person had joined the small group of uniformed cops and she recognized him as Detective Albertson. He finished his short conversation, looked around and noticed her standing by the front door. He made his way up the steps to the two women.

"Welcome back," Leah said.

This seemed to puzzle him for just a moment, and then he smiled. "Yes, I didn't think I'd be back here so soon after seeing the show."

There was an awkward pause, so she shifted the conversation to the social niceties.

"Detective Albertson, this is our Stage Manager, Kanisha," she said quickly. "Kanisha, Detective Albertson was here earlier this week. About the Ronald Hatchet thing. The case. The investigation." She really wasn't clear about the best way to phrase it.

"I'm just helping out Detective Dietz," Albertson said as he put out his hand to Kanisha. She quickly stuffed her tissue back in her sleeve and shook his hand. "Nice to meet you," he continued. "So you've already spoken to the uniformed officers about tonight's incident?"

Kanisha nodded. "They said they would call me if they had any more questions."

"I'm sure they'll follow up," he said, and then turned to Leah. "I'm not here in any official capacity. I just heard the call on the scanner and, having been here so recently, I thought I would swing by. See what's what."

"You don't think the two incidents are connected, do you?" Leah asked. This thought had been lingering in the back of her mind, but she almost felt silly bringing it up.

"Hard to say," Albertson said. "But I'll make sure this team connects with Dietz, just to see if they feel there's any overlap. Are you two okay here?"

"We're fine," Leah said. "We'll just lock up, unless they need anything else?"

Albertson glanced down at the uniformed officers. Their conversation appeared to be breaking up as they headed toward their respective cars.

"No, I think they're good," he said.

"Okay, then we'll lock up. Thanks for updating us," Leah said, as she and Kanisha turned to go into the theater.

"Great show, by the way," Albertson added as he made his way down the front steps. "Very funny. Not sure I was watching the same show as the critic."

"Hatchet," Leah said.

"Yeah, I think he got it wrong," Albertson said. "But then, what do I know?"

"Everyone's a critic. Thanks," Leah said. She watched him go for a few moments longer than necessary. Leah looked over and saw Kanisha was watching her. The two women exchanged a look as they headed back into the building.

"Let's lock up," Leah said.

"Sure thing," Kanisha agreed, smiling for the first time that evening.

* * *

Given the snail's pace at which the theater's Board had moved during her hiring process, Leah was surprised at how quickly they snapped into action after Joan O'Malley's tumble down the back stairs.

An emergency Board meeting was arranged for 10 a.m. the following morning, and despite the short notice and it being a Saturday, nearly the entire Board was assembled when Leah entered the Boardroom.

The room—which felt small with only a handful of people in it—felt absolutely cramped with the nine or ten people assembled. Leah still hadn't memorized all the names but she recognized nearly all the faces.

Of course Gloria was there and she flashed a smile at Leah from her end of the table. Despite the early weekend hour, she was dressed to the nines, somehow managing to look corporate, fashionable and casually chic all at the same time.

Leah also recognized Claudia Moffatt, who had been the Board Member On Duty at the previous night's show. The older woman gave Leah a nod that betrayed nothing positive or negative, just a quick acknowledgment of the younger woman's existence.

Leah also recognized an older gentleman, who she knew was the head of the Play Selection Committee; she thought his name was something like Gavin. She made a mental note to mention the need for more Shaw in the next season. And there was also a young woman who was in charge of the Tech Advisory Committee, whose name was Martina—but again, Leah couldn't pull the last name.

There were other faces she recognized and although she couldn't necessarily recall the names, she could assign almost all of them to the sub-committees they oversaw. There was the guy who ran the Building Committee, the woman who oversaw the Volunteers Committee, and the two people who tag-teamed on the Annual Fundraising Event Committee.

Coming from a much smaller non-profit, Leah was used to working with a comparably smaller Board of Directors. So she was initially overwhelmed by the number of voices and personalities who came along with the larger theater's structure. This was her first full Board Meeting since being hired and only her second time in front of the Board; the first had been at her hiring interview.

Gloria was the current President of the Board and she had done a very good job during the hiring interview, keeping things on track when the occasional digression looked like it would derail the meeting. It might have been her natural leadership ability or the fact that her day job was at the largest regional theater in the Midwest, but when she spoke people tended to listen. And when she told them to stop talking, they usually did.

"Let's get started," Gloria said, her voice cutting through the din in the room.

Leah found a chair by the wall and sat in it. She glanced over at the table to see that Betsy, the theater's Administrative Assistant, had started to take the meeting's notes. Betsy smiled quickly at Leah and then returned her attention to her pad.

"If you're here, that means you read the email about the accident which took place after last night's show," Gloria continued, raising her voice just a bit to silence a two-person conversation at the far end of the table. They stopped talking, looked around sheepishly, and then Gloria continued as if nothing had happened.

"The police are investigating the actor's claim that she was pushed. She is still unconscious, with two broken bones and several contusions, but otherwise doing well at Regions Hospital." Gloria looked around the room. "While it's important that we get to the bottom of this incident, that is not the purpose of today's meeting, and so I request that you table any comments or concerns on that aspect for a later meeting."

All the Board members silently acquiesced, so Gloria glanced down at her notes and then continued.

"Our first order of business has to do with the security cameras we were planning on installing by the front and back doors. I believe we had landed on a vendor and received a bid.

Given the tragic event this past week and the subsequent police investigation, I think it would behoove us to move ahead with that installation as quickly as possible."

Gloria scanned the table quickly until she found the face she was looking for. Leah recognized him as the Chair of the Building Committee.

"Tim, is everything in place to get the cameras installed without delay?" Gloria asked.

Leah looked over at Tim, a man in his mid-fifties who clearly didn't like to have the spotlight shined on him.

"Yes," he stammered as he quickly paged through his notes. "We approved the bid and were planning on installing them once the current show closed. But I can talk to the vendor and get that moved up."

"Let's shoot for Monday," Gloria said and Tim nodded in quick agreement. Gloria glanced down at her notes and then looked up at the group.

"Now, concerning last night's accident. As you all know, it is not the theater's policy to employ understudies for our shows," she said. "All of our positions are unpaid and volunteer. Consequently, it has been decided that asking someone to be an understudy, to commit that much time and effort without the possibility of ever stepping on stage, would be an unreasonable request."

Gloria looked up from her notes. "I'm sure most of you remember the heated debate on that topic, which we are not in a position to revisit today."

Again, the Board members conceded silently, although the woman who ran the Volunteers Committee looked like she really had something to say on this topic. But one look down the table at Gloria persuaded her to stay silent.

"Normally, when an actor is put out of commission and is unable to perform, we have first looked to see if anyone can step into the role. And then, if not, we have canceled.

"For smaller parts, we have even—on occasion—put a new actor on-stage, with book in hand," Gloria continued. "In one noteworthy case, that was our own Gavin Newlund, who bravely filled in at the last minute as the character of the cab driver in the last scene of *Harvey*."

Clearly this was a fond memory for the Board, as it produced several chuckles and some quiet comments directed toward Gavin, who smiled sheepishly and waved them away.

"However, the role of Abby Brewster is too large a role for that approach to work. So normally, in an instance like this, we would likely cancel the run of the show," Gloria said. She looked around the table, making sure she had everyone's attention.

"But this is not a normal circumstance, for two key reasons. For one thing, ticket sales have recently been through the roof on this show. Whether that is connected to the untimely death of Ronald Hatchet or not is a matter of speculation. But the fact is that this show is an unqualified hit. Which is something this theater really, really needs." She paused for emphasis, then turned to Betsy.

"Betsy, just for reference, how often do we sell out the theater?"

Leah could tell the older woman was a bit unnerved by the question. "Um, the number of sellouts, per se, is not—" she began. Gloria recognized Betsy's discomfort and came to her rescue.

"Let me rephrase the question," Gloria said. "What is our average occupancy on a show that's selling well?"

"Oh, if we pass sixty percent of the seats sold, we're doing quite well on a show. Quite well indeed," Betsy said, relieved this new question had been one where she had the answer right at her fingertips.

"And what is our occupancy for the show this weekend, based on last night's show and reservations for tonight and for tomorrow's matinee?" The way Gloria posed the question was like an attorney in court who knows the answer, but just needs it confirmed by the witness.

"Oh, we're at one hundred percent," Betsy said, a bit breathlessly. "If it weren't for those darned fire regulations, it would be even higher."

Gloria ignored this last aside and scanned all the faces at the table. "That's one-hundred percent occupancy for three shows this weekend. Add in the Pay-What-You-Can show on Monday night, and it's clear that we can erase a lot of the theater's financial woes if we can keep this show running this weekend. And beyond."

"But we don't have an actress," Claudia Moffatt said. "No one who can step in at this late date." She gave Gloria a long look, which the Board President returned in her most inscrutable fashion.

"I said this was not a normal situation for two reasons. One was the popularity of this show and the positive impact that might have on the theater's bottom line," Gloria said as she looked at everyone in the room, with the exception of Leah.

It took Leah a moment to recognize this fact, and when she did, she could feel her cheeks starting to turn pink and then red. She saw where this might be headed and didn't like that possible destination.

"As luck would have it," Gloria continued, "we do have—in this very room—an actress who is not only familiar with the role, but who actually *played* Abby Brewster a mere three summers ago."

"Four," Leah said, her voice coming out in a whisper.

"Four summers ago," Gloria repeated. "At the prestigious Westfield Playhouse in Massachusetts."

"The Westport Country Playhouse," Leah corrected. "In Connecticut."

"What she said," Gloria replied, not bothering to repeat the correction. "How fortunate we are that's she's here and willing to do it."

Gloria turned from looking at the others at the table and looked at Leah for the first time since the topic had switched.

"You are willing to do it, aren't you Leah?" Gloria asked. Her tone included an unfamiliar sheen of sweetness to it. "To help out the theater?"

The very idea produced a hubbub of chatter from the other Board members, who were clearly excited at the notion of keeping the show open and reaping the benefits of its newfound popularity.

Leah scanned the faces in the room and saw nothing but smiles shining back at her. With one notable exception.

Claudia Moffatt's expression would best be described as dour or even sour. It wasn't clear if she was adamantly opposed to the idea, but she evidently wasn't thrilled by it.

"There's no way I could get up to speed by tonight," Leah began, searching for a solid reason to turn down the request.

"Oh, we can help you do that," Gloria said, working hard to seal the deal. "Aunt Abby spends half the play off stage and the other half gripping her hymnal. So you've got a handy prop if you need someplace to stash your script. But, knowing what a pro you are," Gloria continued, laying it on a bit thick, "I think the lines will come back faster than you know."

Leah literally couldn't think of a single idea that would get her out of this situation.

"So you'll do it?" Gloria asked.

To Leah, it felt like everyone in the room leaned toward her at the same time.

"I guess so," she said and—as she did—the Board broke into a spontaneous round of applause.

And then, suddenly, everything was happening very quickly.

CHAPTER NINE

"It's just like riding a bike. Except, of course, it's really nothing like riding a bike."

Leah could hear the words being spoken to her by Alex, but they weren't connecting with her brain. She was standing in the center of the large *Arsenic and Old Lace* set, script in hand. Alex was standing next to her and Kanisha had positioned herself in the theater's front row. The Stage Manager had her large binder spread open on her lap.

After the Board meeting had broken up, there had been a bit of a mad scramble to find the right people to help Leah get up to speed on the play. She'd called Kanisha, who immediately nixed the idea of bringing in the entire cast.

"We'd spend the whole day tracking them down," the Stage Manager had said in a reassuring and surprisingly calm voice over the phone. "The only person we need is Alex."

Leah didn't really understand why the actor playing Dr. Einstein would be the ideal person to help walk her through the play's blocking until about five minutes into the impromptu rehearsal. Although his character didn't arrive until near the end of Act One, Alex somehow knew everyone's blocking for just about every moment of the play. And he seemed to know just about everybody's lines as well.

"I get bored," he said by way of explanation. "So I just watch the play and somehow I remember this stuff."

When it came to 'remembering stuff,' Leah was also a bit surprised to discover that Abby's lines were still there, stuffed away in the distant recesses of her brain. The old woman's words weren't exactly top of mind, but when she would hear the cue lines, she found she required fewer and fewer glances at the script in her hands to stir her memory and bring the lines to the surface.

It was slow going during her first scene with the Rev. Dr. Harper, despite the fact that the blocking was relatively simple. She'd make frantic, scribbly notes in her script and then not be able to read them five minutes later. After exiting through the wrong door twice (into the cellar instead of the kitchen), she threw down the script in frustration.

"This is crazy," she said, as she sat dejectedly on the arm of one of the living room's overstuffed chairs. "I can't do this whole play."

"That's not a problem, because you don't ever have to do the whole play," Alex said reassuringly.

"What, are you nuts? Yes I do. And I have to do it tonight!"

Alex shook his head. "You're never doing the whole play," he said. "You're only ever doing the current scene. That's all you ever need to worry about: the current scene. And when that scene is done, you always have off-stage time to review the next scene."

He took her hand and helped her back into a standing position.

"One scene at a time and before you know it, you're at the bar having a drink."

"I may need several drinks before the curtain even goes up."

"In that case, let's run the first scene again." He glanced down at Kanisha.

"Act One, Scene One. Lights up, curtain up!"

Leah and Alex took their places at the table and she spoke

her first lines, which came easier than they had the last time she had spoken them.

"'Yes, indeed, my sister Martha and I have been talking all week about your sermon last Sunday,'" Leah said, becoming more confident the further she got into the line. "'It's really wonderful, Dr. Harper—in only two short years you've taken on the spirit of Brooklyn.'"

* * *

It was slow going, but bit by bit—scene by scene—they made their way through Act One and into Act Two.

Alex was remarkably patient and calm, making her feel like they had all the time in the world, despite Kanisha's unhelpful habit of frequently glancing at her watch. And sighing. And then looking at her watch again.

Alex slipped easily into his Dr. Einstein character when he had lines, but also did fair impressions of just about every other character, making Leah laugh and easing the persistent tension inherent in the task before them. Watching him play both parts– the murderous Jonathan Brewster and the inebriated and starving Dr. Einstein–at the same time was delightful and Leah wished she could spend the whole day just doing that. Unfortunately, she had blocking to learn and lines to re-learn, and so they plowed ahead, further and further into the play. It didn't get easier, but as the afternoon wore on, it at least started to get less terrifying.

They took a short break in the middle of Act Two, sitting quietly on the edge of the stage while Kanisha ran to grab a couple bottles of water and some snacks from the limited inventory found in the vending machines in the kitchen.

This hastily-arranged rehearsal was the first time Leah had really looked at Alex without his Dr. Einstein makeup. She knew he was too young for that part, but she was surprised to realize he was closer to her own age than she had initially thought. His youthful energy—which helped to make his Dr. Einstein so appealing and funny—made him seem younger than his thirty-something years.

"You know, you're a really good actor," Leah said, breaking the unintentional silence they had slowly eased into.

"'She said, with a tone of surprise in her voice,'" Alex joked.

"There was no tone," she countered. "No tone at all. It's just we both know that community theaters can be—"

"A haven for horrible actors?" Alex suggested.

"A mixed bag, actor-wise, was what I was going to say," Leah said. "Did you ever consider turning pro?"

"Well, I'll tell you, my parents really had their hearts set on me making a life in the theater," Alex said. "But you know kids. You can't tell them anything. So I rebelled and got a degree in Accounting instead. I don't think they've ever forgiven me. My father still says to me, 'Remember Alex, if the accounting doesn't work out, at least you have acting to fall back on.'"

Leah laughed. Alex smiled at his ability to have inspired it.

"So that's your day job? You're an accountant?"

"Living the dream, Leah. Living the dream," Alex said. "Jealous?"

"Hey, I'm running a theater with terrific actors like you. What do I have to be jealous about?"

"Oh, you and your flattery."

They exchanged a quick smile which was interrupted by the return of the Stage Manager.

"Okay, I've got two waters," Kanisha said as she headed down the main aisle, her hands filled with bottles and small bags. "Plus some fake potato chips with real cheese and some real potato chips with fake cheese. And, as a bonus, a bag of carbs dipped in sea salt."

"Carbs. Just what I need to make it through the rest of this act," Leah said as she took one of the bottles of water Kanisha was offering.

"You snack, I need to run to the little actor's room," Alex said. "Be right back."

He bounded off the edge of the stage and trotted up the main aisle. Once he had disappeared through the doors to the lobby, Leah turned to Kanisha.

"Do you know, does he like girls?" she asked, trying to make the question sound as casual as possible. She could tell immediately from Kanisha's reaction she had failed.

"Hard to tell with actors," Kanisha said as she looked back toward the lobby. She turned to Leah. "Does it matter?"

"Not in the least," Leah lied as she twisted the cap off her bottled water and took a long sip. She glanced over at Kanisha, but the Stage Manager had returned to her seat and was paging through her ever-present binder.

Leah took another long sip of water and then tore the top off one of the bags of potato chips with cheese, not caring which ingredient was fake and which was real.

By the time they finished running through the entire show—doubling back to re-run a couple problem scenes where Leah kept inverting key lines—there was barely time for her to grab a quick dinner before heading down to the dressing room to prepare for that night's performance.

The show's costumer, Becca, had kindly made a special trip to the theater to make some last-minute alterations on the costumes for Aunt Abby, taking them in to better conform to Leah's slim form.

"With Joan O'Malley, I was aiming for dowdy-chic," Becca explained to Leah, who was standing on a small box while the costumer quickly pinned Abby's Act One dress. "I think I fell short of that mark. But with you, I think we can surpass that and get you all the way to dowdy-sexy."

"That's all I've ever aimed for in real life, so why should it be any different on the stage?" Leah said. She held her script in her hand and was quizzing herself on her Act One, Scene One lines, trying to keep in mind the advice that Alex had imparted: She wasn't doing the whole play, just the current scene.

"Do they have any idea who pushed Joan down the stairs, if that's in fact what happened?" Becca said as she waved Leah off the box and went to grab Abby's dress for Act Three, Scene Two.

"You think she's lying?" Leah said as she unbuttoned the dress and let it fall to the floor.

"I'll say this: I think she's always been overly dramatic and a blamer," Becca said. "I've done a half dozen shows with that woman, and there has been one constant throughout all my travails with her: Nothing is ever her fault. If a cue is missed, it's not her fault. If a prop goes astray, she is the first one to point a finger at someone else. She's like Teflon; nothing sticks. I mean, it's terrible what happened to her, but sometimes we have to take responsibility for our own clumsiness." She had pulled the second dress from the rack. "Back up on the box please."

Leah did as she was told, still paging through her script while she ran lines in her head. But she couldn't help consider Becca's words about whether someone had pushed Joan. Or if Joan was just being Joan.

* * *

"This is sort of funny," Doris said as she looked at Leah's reflection in the makeup mirror they were sharing. "I'm working on taking the age lines off my face, while you're doing just the opposite. Let's hope we can meet somewhere in the middle."

"Don't be silly, you look great," Leah said as she did exactly what the older woman had just pointed out, adding more lines to her forehead.

When Leah had done *Arsenic and Old Lace* four years before, both she and the actress playing Aunt Martha had been in their late twenties. The director's vision had been that both characters were in their mid-forties, which had not been that tough to pull off, makeup-wise.

But in order to appear around the same age as her on-stage sister in this production—who was easily on the far side of sixty–Leah was resorting to more complicated aging makeup. This was adding precious minutes to the rapidly-dwindling time she had between now and the start of the show. She sat back and examined her work.

"It's so nice of you to step in and do this," Doris said as she started the process of pinning her long hair up into Aunt Martha's tight bun.

"If I make it to the end without dropping an entire speech or two, it will be a miracle."

"Don't fret. Joan regularly skips over whole passages. Once she gave me a cue in Act One that she's supposed to say in Act Two," Doris said with a shake of her head. "Of course, she said it was me who said the wrong line, but I really don't think that was the case. I think she just has too many lines to remember."

Leah looked over at the older actress. "You both have about the same number of lines, don't you?" She thought back to her previous production and the balance of lines between the two actresses.

"Oh, heavens no," Doris said with a little laugh. "Martha doesn't even come in until Page 10, and she's much less of a chatterbox than Abby. Of course," she added, leaning in closer to Leah, "I do get the last line in the show. Which is a real treat."

"It's a strong closing line," Leah agreed.

"And that's why Joan tried to take it away from me."

This brought Leah up short. "She did what?"

"She went to the director and made her case that it was more in line with Abby's character to make that little joke. In reality, she just wanted that final laugh." Doris shook her head again, then turned back to the mirror to check her work on securing her bun. "People. Sometimes I just don't get them."

"You and me both," Leah said, surveying her work so far and judging how much time she had left to get into her costume and do another quick review of her first scene. As if to provide that answer, Kanisha sailed through the room.

"Fifteen minutes, people," Kanisha said, not even slowing down.

"Thank you, fifteen minutes," Leah responded by rote, in sync with most of the other actors in the room. She got up and headed to the costume rack.

"If you get a chance," Doris said from her position at the makeup table, "I posted a Get-Well card for Joan over there on the bulletin board. Sign it when you can."

Although she was pressed for time, Leah's curiosity got the better of her and—costume in hand—she made her way to the bulletin board to glance at the card.

Doris had posted the card—with a thumbtack—directly on top of Ronald Hatchet's review of the show. The front of the card, which was drawn in a wildly-colorful caricature style, showed a woman confined to a hospital bed. She looked sad and miserable and the caption read, "The best way to feel better quick..."

Leah opened the card revealed the punch line: "...is to get your nurse to fill your IV bag with a martini!" This was accompanied by a drawing of the IV bag, with two green olives floating in it. At the bottom of the image, was the final greeting: "Get Well Soon and Hurry Back to Us!"

Leah looked at the card again, which was free of notes or signatures.

"I don't want to be the first," she said as she turned back to Doris.

"That's what everybody has said," Doris replied with a weary smile and a sad shake of her head. "But I think the truth is, no one believes in the message."

Leah reread the printed message ("Get Well Soon and Hurry Back to Us!"). Based on what she had seen and heard so far about Joan O'Malley and her treatment of her fellow actors, she understood the reluctance of other cast members to sign the card. It was as if they were thinking that the very act of signing the get-well greeting would summon the dreaded woman back faster than if they didn't sign it. So no one signed it.

A pen hung on a string from another thumbtack. Leah grabbed it, thought for a moment, and then wrote a quick message on the card ("Best wishes for a speedy recovery!") and then signed her name under it.

She then headed into the women's dressing room to pull on her costume, lace up her shoes, and then head up to the stage for what was rapidly feeling like the most terrifying performance of her acting career.

CHAPTER TEN

"Okay, Sound C and Lights Three–go," Kanisha said quietly into her headset, although whispering wasn't actually required in this instance. The tech booth at the back of the auditorium was not completely soundproof, but close enough. However she still whispered out of long habit. "Standby for Light Cue Four."

The light board operator followed her instructions, lowering the house lights in the auditorium to half, while the kid running the sound board faded out the walk-in music. This provided the audience with the visual and audio cues they needed to tell them the show was about to begin. The hubbub in the room began to diminish at about the same percentage as the lights had.

"Lights Four. Go," Kanisha said, silently praying that the Board Member on Duty was standing by to step on-stage. She had made eye contact with him less than two minutes before, but just like baby ducks, Board Members on Duty (BMODs, as everyone called them) had a really annoying tendency to sometimes wander off.

She need not have worried.

Gavin Newlund had positioned himself by the stage left steps and as soon as he recognized the house lights were dimming, he began to make his way to the steps and up onto the stage. He hit the platform just as the special light came up in front of the curtain, and moments later he was standing on the pieces of white glow tape which formed a small "x" on the stage. This was his mark, and he hit it like a pro. He knew to avoid the lip of the stage, which was tough to see under the lights. So tough that more than one BMOD before him had tumbled off the stage in mid-speech.

"Good evening," he said, before the smattering of applause had a chance to grow to anything larger. "Good evening and welcome to the Como Lake Players production of *Arsenic and Old Lace*."

The people who had wanted to applaud earlier saw an opening here and started to clap for the title of the play, which led others in the audience to join in. Gavin waited for this small ovation to die down.

"I'm Gavin Newlund and I'm on the Board of Directors here at the theater. I have just a couple quick notes to go over before the start of tonight's show."

With that, he launched into the standard BMOD speech about cell phones *(turn them off)*, number of intermissions *(just one)*, where the bathrooms were *(in the lobby)*, and how to buy season tickets *(see me during intermission)*.

Unlike some of the other BMODs, Gavin had customized this presentation, including a joke about pagers *("Hey, 1990 called and they want your pager back")*, as well some historical trivia about the current show. *("Yes, it's true, Boris Karloff himself appeared in the original Broadway production of this show. I'll leave it to you to guess just which character he played!")*

Gavin had done some acting back in college and even performed a few small parts at this theater, including his legendary save as the cab driver in *Harvey*. Consequently, he felt more confident than many of the Board Members when it came to doing this traditional pre-show BMOD speech. Plus it never hurt to warm up the crowd with a couple well-placed laughs, and he had already proven that task was certainly well within his wheelhouse.

In fact, he was confident he still had one or two more laughs in him tonight, and so he plowed forward.

* * *

"Can anyone say *loquacious*?" Kanisha said to no one in particular as she glanced at her watch. She quickly calculated how late the first act intermission would be if he kept talking. She looked up as it began to sound like he might be wrapping up.

"One last thing," he said, holding up one finger to reinforce the idea that it really was only going to be this one thing.

"Due to an accident after last night's show, the actress who normally plays Abby Brewster will not be able to perform tonight. But, in her place, we are very pleased to announce that the role of Abby Brewster will be played tonight by none other than our own new Executive Director, Leah Sexton."

This announcement produced a mix of applause and confused conversation throughout the audience. Gavin nodded at the response, and looked like he was about to say something else. But before he could, Kanisha had already called the cue to start the show.

The stage lights dimmed to black and the opening music began as Gavin scrambled off the stage and up the aisle to his seat in the back row. Like everyone else, he was really curious about how tonight's show would go with an untested and essentially unrehearsed actress. He wasn't hoping for the worst, but if the show was going to go down in flames, he didn't want to be the guy who missed seeing it.

* * *

"Break a leg."

Leah heard this classic whispered encouragement, and many other variations, several times as she made her way from the Green Room to her entrance point backstage. Stuart Wilde, the actor who played Rev. Dr. Harper, was already standing by their entrance, peering through a crack in the doorway as he listened to Gavin Newlund provide the pre-show BMOD speech.

"This one is in love with the sound of his own voice," Stuart whispered to Leah as she took her place next to him. She nodded as she gave her costume one final tug of adjustment and then reached up to make sure her wig had not become mussed in the short walk up the steep flight of stairs. The same stairway, she remembered with a shudder, that Joan O'Malley had tumbled down less than twenty-four hours before.

Leah was relieved that she and Stuart had found time to do a quick run-through of their lines for the opening scene. Unfortunately, they'd had to leave gaps for the lines of Teddy Brewster, as that actor had arrived too late to take part in their impromptu rehearsal.

She saw him now—was it Teddy? Eddie? That was it, his name was Eddie but everyone called him Teddy—as he rushed over to their entrance point and made a few minor adjustments to his frock coat and pince-nez. He did really look a lot like Teddy Roosevelt, Leah thought. Before she could say anything to him, the Assistant Stage Manager swung the door open and they scrambled into the dark, following the glow tape on the floor to their places on the blackened stage.

The lights, when they came up, nearly blinded Leah as she picked up a tea cup and handed it, shakily, to the Rev. Dr. Harper. He took the cup and saucer and held it a second longer than necessary, to help steady her wobbling hand.

She looked from his eyes to Teddy's eyes. Both men seemed to be smiling and nodding, waiting patiently for the first line of the play. Or, she felt, the first line of *any* play. Clearly they wanted—needed—her to say something. She could have launched into *The Iceman Cometh* and they would have looked relieved–at least for a few seconds.

"'*Yes, indeed, my sister Martha and I have been talking all week about your sermon last Sunday,*'" Leah finally said, her voice growing in volume and confidence as she made her way through her first lines. *"'It's really wonderful, Dr. Harper—in only two short years you've taken on the spirit of Brooklyn.'"*

That was all it took and suddenly they were off and running. Leah willed herself to stay in the moment, stay in the scene, and only concern herself with the next line. And then the next line after that.

And, she was amazed to discover, each line was coming to her—often just in time, but thankfully it was there–as the play hurled forward. She felt like she was on a speeding train and the only thing to do was to hang on for dear life. And so she did.

Cast members peered through the thin cracks in the set during the opening scene, marveling as Leah executed the most frightening of all actor nightmares: Being thrown on stage with little or no rehearsal.

"So far, so good," Monica whispered.

"She's getting the lines <u>and</u> she's getting laughs," Lucas said, a tone of awe in his voice.

"She's a pro," Alex said as he felt a tinge of pride at how well Leah was doing and the oh-so small part he had played in that success. "An absolute pro."

"I know this is a terrible thing to say," Doris whispered to anyone who might be listening, "but better her than me. I could never attempt such a feat. Not when I was her age. And certainly not now."

"You might surprise yourself," Alex said, trying to decide if it was okay to give the older woman's back a pat and then opting against it. "You just never know," he added as he returned his attention to the miraculous juggling act Leah was performing on stage. It was the most dramatic thing any of them had seen in years.

* * *

"She's doing great," Gavin Newlund said in an exaggerated *sotto voce* from his seat at the rear of the auditorium. "Just great."

Four house seats in the back row were always reserved for

Board members and while some nights three of the chairs sat empty, tonight they were full.

"I never doubted her," Gloria whispered in return, although inside she was breathing a huge sigh of relief. She'd known her idea had been a crapshoot and was glad to see that—at the top of Act One, at least—her friend seemed to be pulling it off.

"She's so brave," Martine Lopez said, watching as Aunt Abby cheerfully invited Officers Brophy and Klein into the Brewster's living room. There was a little blocking confusion on their entrance—with Aunt Abby going upstage of them, rather than downstage as planned—but the actors played it all like a natural human interaction and the audience was none the wiser.

"We shall see," Claudia Moffatt mumbled to herself, although loud enough to be heard by her seat mates.

Gloria looked over at her fellow Board Member. She noticed Claudia was clenching her program so firmly that it had become a crumpled mess in her tight fist. Before she could consider this further, her attention was drawn back to the stage, where Aunt Abby was making her first exit.

"I won't be a minute." Leah said with as much sweetness as she could muster to the two policeman. *"Sit down and be comfortable, all of you."* And with that she scurried over to the door on her left, at the last second favoring it over the door on her right.

"Darling, that was fantastic," Doris whispered as Leah burst into the dim backstage area. Doris was just heading across to the far doorway, the one the police had just entered through. "Just perfection."

"The cellar door and the kitchen door were reversed in the production I was in," Leah explained, although nothing had seemed amiss about her exit. "I can never remember which is which. I'm terrified I'll go through the wrong door."

But Doris was already gone, moving to the front door to make her first appearance in the play. Leah made a dive to the table where she had left her script, paging ahead frantically to her next entrance and the words that were expected to come out of her mouth.

"I think it's going very well," Monica whispered to Leah, who was running her finger across her lines, giving the impression she was desperately trying to absorb the words directly through her skin. Which wasn't really all that far from the truth.

"I'm sorry?" Leah said, looking up at the young woman.

"I didn't mean to disturb you," Monica said, backing away. "I play Elaine. Elaine Harper. I'll see you on-stage. In just a few minutes."

Leah watched the young woman retreat further into the backstage murk, and then turned her attention back to the lines. There were *so* many lines. So, so many lines. And she had to make all of them come out of her mouth, at the right time and in the right order.

Cursing her parents for allowing her to become an actor in the first place, she returned her attention to the next scene and the ungodly torrent of words she was expected to say.

As she crawled her way through each scene, Leah realized that Alex's advice—to be in the moment and only worry about the current scene—was probably saving her life.

While the process wasn't exactly *fun*, once she got into the rhythm, it wasn't as painful as she thought it would be. For his part, Alex stayed out of her way during her brief backstage breaks, but they exchanged quick smiles at one point as Leah dropped her script and headed back on stage.

Alex—all decked out in his Dr. Einstein wig and mustache–gave her a thumbs up, and Leah returned it before pushing open the door and stepping back into the play.

"Oh, you're back, Martha," Leah said, proudly remembering to look over at Doris as she delivered this line. *"How was Mr. Benitzky?"*

And just like that, the two old sisters were conversing away, as if they'd been doing exactly that for years and years, easily mixing talk of murder and the neighborhood children, as if each topic was as normal as the other.

Leah breezed through her first scene with Martha and then the longer scene with Elaine and finally Mortimer.

They were a cute couple, although to Leah, the actor playing Mortimer seemed stiff compared to the loosey-goosey line readings Elaine was giving. She remembered that someone had mentioned the two were currently dating, which took her back to her previous production of this play. In her summer stock experience, it had been Mortimer and Teddy who were dating off-stage.

In many ways, the entire experience was giving her an overwhelming and uncanny sense of *deja vu*: the words and actions were familiar, but the people and the setting were not quite what she remembered.

She and Doris exited together, leaving Elaine and Mortimer *(was it Monica and Lucas, Leah thought? Yes, she thought that were their names)* on-stage for their extended Act One scene.

While Doris went to get a sip of water, Leah immediately dove back into her script, looking at the long scene that lay ahead of her.

Once she re-entered, she would be on-stage—with only a couple very short trips into the kitchen—until the end of the act. The only saving grace was that Alex would be showing up soon, which was a comforting thought.

But she still had lots and lots of lines to get through before that would occur.

* * *

Her next scene—with Aunt Martha and nephew Mortimer—went pretty well, although Leah missed two cues and forgot to pick up one prop.

But it was invisible to the audience, as Doris quickly took up the slack. The other actress covered for Leah's first-night gaffs by providing the lines that Abby needed to say at that point and kept the story moving forward.

Alex finally arrived as Dr. Einstein and his appearance brought Leah a strong sense of relief. She was off-stage briefly during his entrance with Jonathan Brewster, but once she made it back into the living room set, she began to have a little fun for the first time that evening.

There were a lot of laughs in the scene, with the two creepy men contrasting sharply with the two dotty women, each working hard to hold their respective ground.

The banter back and forth was fun and Leah got the sense—a feeling she hadn't had watching earlier performances of the play—that Dr. Einstein was just shy of flirting with Aunt Abby. At first she thought it was her imagination, but the way Dr. Einstein (or Alex) looked at her had a funny, almost smirking quality to it.

Leah was just about to say one of her favorite lines *("We're very fond of Mortimer"),* because she remembered that in the production five years before, she could get a laugh if she started the line while looking directly at Jonathan Brewster and then turning away while saying it.

She did just that, turning from Jonathan and looking right into the audience. And that's when she saw him.

Leah knew she was supposed to look pale and frightened in this scene and now she was sure she had nailed it.

He was seated in the front row, looking up at her.

It was her ex-boyfriend.

It was him.

It was Dylan.

CHAPTER ELEVEN

Somehow Leah made it to the intermission.

It had been a huge help that she'd been playing the scene with Alex when she spotted Dylan in the audience. And it didn't hurt that Doris seemed to have a solid grasp on the lines for both Aunt Martha <u>and</u> Aunt Abby, because for several long seconds, every word Leah ever knew left her head.

Seeing Dylan smiling up at her from the front row was such a total and unwelcome surprise, that Leah continued to have real trouble remembering the lines as the scene barreled forward. It probably helped that her character was supposed to be addled and terrified throughout this section. Leah felt that she absolutely nailed those emotions and maybe a little more.

Her exit came about thirty seconds before the curtain fell, as she and Martha headed into the kitchen. She said the first part of her final line *("Oh yes. Just as he left it.")* but when she tried to continue, she found the second part of the line was nowhere in her brain.

Luckily, Doris picked up the slack, taking the line *"Well, I'll help Martha get things started—since we're all in a hurry,"* and simply swapped out *"Martha"* for *"Abby."* She then ushered Leah off the stage, through the kitchen door–Leah was halfway to the cellar door when Doris grabbed her–and into the safety of the backstage area.

Leah collapsed into a chair, next to the small rickety table she'd been using for her quick script reviews. Next to the script was her cell phone. She grabbed it and–as she could hear the audience applauding the end of the act–quickly typed a short message.

The message read: *Dylan is here. Help!*

Then Leah hit SEND.

* * *

The makeup area and Green Room were abuzz with movement and adrenaline, as actors rushed about to prepare themselves for the second half of the play. For some of them this meant full costume changes, for others just a quick brush-up on their makeup.

For Leah it meant all of that, plus continued frantic study of the seemingly *hundreds* of lines she still had to say that evening. While a few of the cast members offered their congratulations to her for making it through Act One, most maintained a respective distance. They recognized the arduous task ahead of her and didn't want to throw her off or unnecessarily break her concentration.

But she knew her concentration was not just broken but utterly shattered. And the reason for it was one simple word.

Dylan.

Her phone vibrated on the makeup table next to her script and she saw the response Gloria had sent to her frantic text.

Don't panic. On my way.

Too late, Leah thought as she glanced at the phone's screen. She had been in panic mode since that morning's Board meeting. The appearance of Dylan had elevated that level of panic from DEFCON 3 to DEFCON 5.

Leah did her best to push all the Dylan anxiety out of her mind and instead focus her seemingly boundless angst on the energy and concentration she would need to summon for the second half of the play.

She was not as successful at this as she would have liked.

* * *

Gloria read Leah's message just as she was paying for the glass of white wine she had ordered at the concession stand.

As the President of the Board, she had fought hard for the theater to obtain the necessary licensing to offer beer and wine at intermission. It was, she argued, not only a nice benefit for their customers, but also a robust profit center for a theater which had precious few other ways to bring in much-needed extra income.

It had required obtaining a special license from the city and an appearance before the City Council, along with producing letters of support from the theater's neighbors. Gloria had undertaken this arduous task herself, telling one and all that it was for the good of the theater and its patrons. But she had also overcome all those obstacles simply because, on those nights when she attended a play as the President of the Como Lake Players' Board of Directors, she wanted to have the option to enjoy a glass of wine–or two–at intermission.

While she was immensely proud of the work she had put into this cause, her first sip of the pale wine reminded her that the battle was far from over. They simply had to stock a Chablis that didn't taste like a watered-down wine cooler. She was making a mental note to bring that up at the next Board meeting when she saw Leah's text.

"Oh my," Gloria said quietly as she scanned the short text. "What fresh hell is this?"

Gloria had only met Dylan once before, on a quick weekend trip to New York. She had recognized immediately that this a-little-too-attractive guy was going to be problematic for Leah. Gloria knew that the moment he welcomed her with a surprising, probing kiss rather than a quick handshake. She had seen his type before; in fact, she had dated that type all through college, before the sheer weight of the heartaches had helped her to wise up.

As compelling as a Dylan could be—great looks, hot body, highly passionate—the downside to that upside could be brutal, as both she and Leah had learned.

Gloria glanced at the text again and typed a quick response, then turned her attention to scanning the intermission crowd mingling through the lobby and roaming around the concession stand. She was pretty sure she would recognize Dylan if she saw him, but wasn't nearly as certain that he would recognize her. For now, she hoped he wouldn't.

Gloria took another sip of the nearly tasteless wine as she moved through the crowd, her eyes straining for any sign of him as she made her way toward the stairs to the Green Room. She was just reaching for the door handle when she spotted him.

It had been several years, but those years had clearly been good to Dylan. He was one of those guys who started out cute and then, amazingly, evolved into handsome, losing none of the sexiness along the way. His dishwater blonde hair was swept back in a calculated but casual unkempt wave, while the lines around his sparkling blue eyes simply made them shine a little brighter. And he still had the damned dimples, his cheekbones having lost none of their sharp and sensual contours.

Gloria recognized at once that she was not the only one looking at Dylan. And she also realized that he knew this and counted on it as a daily occurrence. There were people in the world who looked and people who were looked at, and Dylan was at the top of the heap of that latter category.

As he moved, oh-so casually through the room, the words of that Carly Simon song, *You're So Vain*, started running in her head.

"You had one eye in the mirror and something about gavotting, whatever that meant," she thought as she watched him parade across the lobby. He looked just as good walking away from her as he had coming toward her, and Gloria knew that meant trouble.

She made a lunge for the door handle and moments later was through the door and on her way down to the Green Room.

* * *

"Did you see him?"

Gloria nodded, taking the final sip from her feeble wine. "You know, we have to talk about the quality of this wine. It's so watery, it tastes like Jesus was interrupted halfway through his miracle."

"You saw him?" Leah said again, her mind a million miles away from what brand of wine the theater needed to stock for resale. "Dylan? It's him?"

Gloria nodded again, looking for a surface on which to put her now empty wine glass. "Oh, it's definitely him," she said as Leah impatiently snatched the glass from her and set it on the makeup table.

"You're sure?"

"Well, I only met him that one weekend when I visited you, but yes, I'm sure it's Dylan."

"I only got a glimpse of him, the lights were in my eyes. How does he look?" Leah asked quietly, wishing she didn't feel the need to pose that question and really not wanting to hear the answer. Unless the answer was that he looked terrible. That was an answer she would love to hear.

Gloria shut her eyes, just for a second as Leah awaited her judgment. After a few seconds Gloria opened her eyes and shook her head sadly.

"I wish I could say he wasn't still gorgeous, but I can't lie," she said. "Dylan has successfully eluded the ravages of time."

"Gloria, I just saw him three months ago," Leah said. "I really didn't expect him to have gained forty pounds and go bald in that time. I just meant, did he look sad. Or lost. Or, I don't know, sorry that he's such a schmuck?"

"To be honest, the short look I got of his face didn't suggest any of those emotions," Gloria said. "But, judging from how he looked walking away, he must be doing Pilates. Or squats or lunges or something."

"Sometimes you are no help whatsoever," Leah said as she turned back to give her makeup one last check in the mirror.

"Five minutes, people," Kanisha barked as she cruised through the room. "Five minutes."

"Thank you, five minutes," Leah said, in unison with the rest of the cast.

"Look, let's do this," Gloria said as she leaned in to give her own makeup the once-over in the mirror. She pulled a lipstick out of her purse and coated her lips expertly. "I'll go back up and see if I can casually bump into Dylan. You know, 'Oh, I thought you looked familiar,' that sort of thing. Chat him up. Find out why he's here. And then I can report back to you at the end of the show."

"That's all well and good, but I don't want to see him," Leah said with a shudder. "Not tonight, not this weekend. Probably not ever, but certainly not tonight."

She gently pushed Gloria away from the mirror so that she could complete her own makeup check and get her wig back on. She glanced down and saw her script, opened to Act Two, with all her illegible chicken scratches in the margins. "Oh my god, I still have half a play to do," she said, snatching at the wig and jamming it on her head. "Why tonight of all nights?"

"Don't you worry," Gloria said as she grabbed one of Leah's tissues off the table to blot her lipstick. "I'll take care of Dylan and we'll deal with smuggling you out later. You just go do that acting thing."

Gloria straightened up and then turned back. "Break a leg," she said, and then realized the implications of that phrase in this particular situation. "And I don't mean like the actress last night," she added.

"I got it, I got it," Leah said, waving her away and turning her attention back to the makeup mirror. "But to be honest, being in the hospital with a concussion and two broken legs is starting to look like a day at the beach right about now."

* * *

The overhead lights were just being flicked on and off as Gloria completed the hike up the stairs and made her way back into the lobby.

About half the crowd immediately began rushing back to their seats, demonstrating a Pavlovian-like response to the standard signal that intermission was nearly over.

The other half of the crowd either ignored the flickering lights or realized they still had a few minutes to mosey back into the theater, because the play was unlikely to start again with half the audience still in the lobby.

Gloria scanned the horde, looking for Dylan's mop of dirty blonde hair above the mostly gray and blue hair visible in the crowd. He wasn't immediately evident. To get a better view, she moved over to the stairway that led up to the tech booth, positioning herself on the second step. From this higher perch, she still had no luck spotting Leah's wayward ex-boyfriend and ex-business partner.

Kanisha, who had engineered the flickering of the lobby lights, slipped past her on her way back up the short set of stairs to her work station. Gloria nodded at the young Stage Manager as she passed.

"Well, that was a bit of unexpected excitement," Kanisha commented as she made her way up toward the booth.

"It certainly was," Gloria agreed and then realized she had no idea what Kanisha was talking about. She turned and looked up the stairs. "What excitement?"

But Kanisha had already disappeared through the door into the tech booth. Gloria turned back toward the lobby and her fruitless search for the elusive Dylan, immediately forgetting the short exchange with the young woman.

Gloria was one of the last to take her seat, as she'd spent the remaining few moments before the play began again, craning her neck from various locations throughout the lobby. None had provided her with the pay-off she had desired. So, as she got to her seat, she stood on tiptoe to see if she could see Dylan's signature shock of blonde-ish hair in the front row.

"What a surprising turn of events," Gavin Newlund whispered to her as she finally settled into her seat.

Martina, on her other side, echoed Gavin's mood. "I certainly didn't expect to see that," she agreed. "Not in a million years."

"Okay, what's going on?" Gloria said, doing nothing to soften the tone of exasperation in her voice. "I was downstairs for like eight minutes, tops. What in god's name did I miss, for crying out loud?"

"The police were here," Martina said, her voice slipping into a whisper as the lights began to dim.

"The police?" Gloria repeated.

"They came in during intermission," Gavin explained, turning so he could speak quietly to her. "Asked for her by name, talked to her for a couple of minutes in the lobby, and then escorted her out to a patrol car."

"Asked for who by name?" Gloria snapped, wondering why it was so impossible for these two dingbats to get to any actual point.

"Claudia Moffatt," Gavin said. "They're taking her in to question her. On suspicion of Ronald Hatchet's murder."

As luck would have it, Gloria's response–which was loud and deeply profane–was drowned out by the audience's applause as the curtain rose and the play once again resumed on stage.

CHAPTER TWELVE

Leah, of course, was blissfully unaware of the incident between Claudia Moffatt and the police which had taken place during intermission—although she probably would not have employed 'blissful' as an accurate description of her current state of mind. Her brain was still scrambled, but only a little less so.

The second act opened with Abby and Martha on-stage with Jonathan Brewster and Dr. Einstein, so Leah had the benefit of starting the scene with Alex already on-stage. This fact—and Doris' innate skill at picking up any lines Leah might inadvertently drop—helped her ease into the second half of the play. She had a degree of calmness—a small one, to be sure, but it was there—which she hadn't possessed going into Act One.

One of the reasons for this might have been because, throughout the second half of the play, Leah made a point of <u>never</u> looking at the front row. She simply didn't want to confirm or reconfirm Dylan was sitting there, silently watching and judging her. She'd already had more than enough of that from him in her life; it was one of the major reasons she had left him and left New York.

Leah had realized early-on in her relationship with Dylan that he wasn't really a huge fan of her as an actress; the very few compliments he had offered over their five years together had always felt backhanded and passive-aggressive in nature.

She remembered one instance when he'd told a group of assembled colleagues that he thought "Leah really should explore soap opera acting, as I think she'd do quite well in that end of the business." When she'd pressed him on it later, he said he was simply referring to her unique skill of being able to memorize a great deal of dialog in a short amount of time–obviously a necessary talent for soap opera actors.

But Leah had never really bought this explanation. In fact, in her heart, she felt—when it came to her career as an actress–Dylan hadn't truly really believed she'd amount to much of anything.

"Why would he ever think something like that?" she mused when she allowed her mind to wander briefly during a short monologue by Jonathan Brewster. "Look how far I've come: From acting in New York and Off-Broadway all the way to being a last-minute stand-in at a community theater in St. Paul."

Leah only allowed herself this one moment of self-pity before diving back into the scene, as Abby and Martha tried their hardest to rid themselves of their two pesky houseguests. Leah continued to maintain this focus throughout the rest of the act. While it wasn't exactly what she would call fun, it did go by without a significant hitch.

The only time she allowed herself to look into the audience–and in particular, at the front row–was during the curtain call. It wasn't during her individual bow, which she was pleased to discover received a fair amount of ovation from the audience.

Instead, she took a moment to glance at the front row while she and the entire cast were assembled on-stage for their final, group bow. At that moment, she permitted herself one quick peek at where Dylan was sitting.

But he wasn't there.

His seat was empty. She continued with the final bow, but also scanned the aisles, to see if he was making a quick run for the exit.

But he was nowhere in sight. And, as far as she knew, he hadn't even been there at all for the second half of the show.

"Great," she thought as she moved backstage with the rest of the cast, headed to the stairs. "Not only does he show up out of nowhere the first time I'm on stage in Minnesota, but then he doesn't even bother to stay for the whole show."

She realized she was feeling a lot of mixed emotions, but figured that was to be expected at the end of a long day and an even longer performance.

"He was there in the lobby during intermission, before I came downstairs. But I saw no sign of him after I came back from talking to you," Gloria said. "And from my seat in the rear of the auditorium, I couldn't see whether or not he was in the front row before the second half started."

"Do you think he might have ducked out early, during the curtain call?"

Gloria shook her head. "I was sitting right in the back row, with a clear view of both aisles. I didn't see him."

Leah thought about this for a long moment. She was back in her makeup chair, undoing all the work she had done to get herself ready to play the aged Aunt Abby. "But you're sure you saw him at intermission? And that it was really Dylan?" For the first time, she was beginning to doubt herself about whether or not she'd actually seen him in the front row.

"Yes, hon, I'm sure it was him. Dylan has many rotten qualities, but he is—at his core—memorable."

"He is that," Leah agreed and then she turned her head with a sudden motion. She turned back, moving her head slowly from side to side. She closed her eyes.

"What are you doing?" Gloria asked. "Some weird new neck exercises?"

"It's Dylan," Leah said quietly. "Or at least his cologne. For just a second, I thought I smelled his cologne." She turned her head again slowly, right to left, and then shook her head. "It must have been my imagination."

Gloria was about to respond, but suddenly they were set

upon by a couple of the older actors who pushed past her to get to Leah.

"Outstanding work," Clyde Henderson said in his odd, almost-British accent. "Just first rate."

He turned to Stuart Wilde, who was still sporting the collar he wore as Rev. Dr. Harper. Stuart put his hand on his heart and recited a limerick composed just for this occasion.

"Dear Leah, when asked to play Abby / Adopted the role without being crabby / She stepped in–in a pinch / Knocked them dead–in a cinch / With a performance that wasn't too shabby."

Leah laughed and gave him a small round of applause. Stuart and Clyde continued into the dressing room, but before Gloria could comment, the actor playing Officer Brophy stopped on his way past them.

"Congratulations," he said as he unbuttoned his patrolman costume. "Just an amazing performance. Never seen anything like it!"

"Well that's very kind of you to say," Alex said. He had suddenly appeared next to Brophy and was also headed to the men's dressing room. "But how about a nice word for Leah?"

"That was for Leah, you moron," Brophy said, looking down at Leah with a 'can you believe this guy?' look before continuing on his way.

"Good work, kid," was all Alex said, giving her a smile and a wink. He had pulled off the Dr. Einstein wig and was tugging on the mustache as he rounded the corner to his own makeup chair.

"Thanks," Leah said, and then turned back to Gloria, who was taking a long look at the muscled physique of Officer Brophy–now down to just his t-shirt as he stood in the doorway to the dressing room. Leah snapped her fingers at her friend. "Pay attention," she said sharply.

"Sorry," Gloria said, although they both knew she wasn't in the least bit sorry. She craned her neck to take one more look.

Leah rolled her eyes at her. "And what about this other thing? You said the police took Claudia Moffatt away during the intermission?"

"That's what they tell me," Gloria said. "I'm really sorry I missed it, too. If there is one person in the world I've always wanted to see in a handcuffed-perp-walk, it's Claudia Moffatt. I'm so bummed that I missed it!"

"Maybe one of the patrons filmed it with their phone and you can find it online."

"A person can only hope."

"Why do the police think Claudia was involved with Hatchet's murder? And why wait five days to do anything about it? And why do it during a live performance at the theater?"

"Those are all excellent questions," Gloria said. "I think to find the answers to one or all of them, we need to get some assistance from a professional."

"A professional?" Leah said as she looked up at her friend.

"A professional gossip," Gloria explained, taking one more long, lusty look at Brophy in his t-shirt before he disappeared for good into the men's dressing room. "Finish up here and we'll go talk to her."

* * *

"Well, it's really not my place to say," Betsy said from behind her cluttered desk. She had finished tallying the night's receipts and was filling out a deposit slip, in anticipation of her stop at the after-hours depository at the bank on her way home.

"Let's make it your place," Gloria said warmly as she perched on the edge of the older woman's desk. "We're all friends here."

Betsy looked up at her and then glanced at the door to her small office. She gave Leah a quick, knowing nod. It took a moment, but then Leah understood the body language and quietly shut the door.

"Well, I have no proof of course, except what I saw with my own two eyes," she said in an almost comic stage whisper. "But I've heard rumors that corroborate what I saw. So if it's not the absolute truth, it's the closest thing to it."

"What did you see?" Leah asked and then immediately recognized the shocked look on Betsy's face. She repeated the question, this time carefully mimicking the older woman's whisper. "What did you see?"

"It was back when we were doing *The Odd Couple*," she said, her voice dipping even lower in volume. Leah stepped forward to better hear the octogenarian as she breathlessly recounted her story.

"We were done for the night and I was just heading to my car in the parking lot. It was a dark night, cloudy, without much moonlight. I walked past what I thought was an empty car, but then for some reason–at the very moment I passed by–the dome light in the car came on. And I realized it *wasn't* an empty car. Not by a long shot."

Betsy was recounting her tale as if she were unspooling a ghost story around a summer campfire. While Leah appreciated the attempt at drama, she silently wished that the point–any point–could be reached soon.

"And who do you think I see, canoodling in the front seat of the car?" Betsy continued. Leah wasn't sure if the question was rhetorical or not. She also wasn't entirely certain of the correct definition of *canoodling*.

"Canoodling?" she repeated, but Gloria waved it away.

"Necking. Smooching, Snogging," Gloria said quickly, rattling off the words. "You know: kissing."

"Ah," Leah said, finally catching onto the colloquialism.

"Who did you see?" Gloria asked as she turned back to Betsy.

"Well, it wasn't the brightest light in the world, that dome light," Betsy said. "Not like the one in my station wagon, which is like turning on the sun, way too bright, if you ask me."

"And who did you see?" Gloria repeated, making an 'okay, let's move along here' gesture with her hands.

"It was Claudia Moffatt. And that critic, Roland Hatchet. They were too...*involved*...to notice me," Betsy said, making the word 'involved' sound like the most salacious of *double entendres*.

"And then, just like that, the dome light snapped off. And I couldn't see a thing inside the dark car."

Gloria considered this for a long moment. "Talk about an odd couple," she mused, still considering this new information.

Leah looked at the two women. "Maybe I'm missing something here, but why is this a big deal? They're both adults, right? Were they married to other people or something or what?" Leah's voice trailed off as her question ran out of steam.

Gloria and Betsy exchanged a look, and then Gloria turned to Leah. "Over the years there has been no bigger critic of that critic–Ronald Hatchet–than Claudia Moffat," Gloria explained. "She hated him with the burning intensity of a thousand suns."

"She did not like that man," Betsy agreed with a sad shake of her head.

"Claudia even proposed a serious resolution to the Board that Hatchet be banned from the theater," Gloria continued. "For life."

"It nearly passed, too," Betsy said ruefully. "But, thankfully, calmer heads prevailed."

"Banned for life? Because of some negative reviews?" Leah asked.

"No, because of his *consistently* negative reviews," Gloria replied. "No other critic in town has panned our shows more than Ronald Hatchet. It was like an obsession for him, like an addiction: 'What's the meanest thing I can say about the latest show at the Como Lake Players?'"

Betsy nodded. "He's written some really mean things. Or did write. Wrote."

Gloria turned back to Betsy. "So this finally explains his review for *The Odd Couple*."

"He panned that show, too?" Leah said.

"On the contrary," Gloria said. "His review for *The Odd Couple* was glowing. A rave. A flat-out boffo review."

"And he was pretty positive about the next two shows, as well," Betsy added.

"And then, just like that," Gloria said as she snapped her fingers. "We were back to being panned. Again and again."

"Until this week," Leah suggested.

Gloria narrowed her eyes. "What do you mean? He panned this show too."

"I know," Leah said. "But clearly that's the last time Ronald Hatchet will ever pan a show–ours or anyone else's–again."

"True enough. But the question I'm guessing the police are asking right now is," Gloria said slowly, "given her past relationship with him, what role did Claudia Moffatt play in his death?"

Her question hung in the air, unanswered for several seconds. Gloria finally spoke again, this time so loudly and suddenly that Betsy actually jumped a little in her chair.

"This calls for some deep thought over a glass of wine."

With that, she was out the door. Leah bade a quick goodnight to Betsy and then followed her friend out of the small office.

CHAPTER THIRTEEN

Leah had always been greatly amused that just about every one of Gloria's best stories undoubtedly began with her saying, "So, I'm having a glass of wine, when all of a sudden ..."

Leah was reminded of this as she sat across the table from her old friend in Jimmy's bar, across the street from the theater. Gloria, of course, already had a glass of wine in her hand. It was her second. She scanned the large room thoughtfully while she sipped.

"I'm dying to know what the police are asking Claudia Moffatt," she finally said. "If only we could be a fly on that wall."

Leah nodded in agreement as she wiped a smudge from the rim of her own wine glass. And then a thought occurred to her. She set down the glass and began to dig through her purse.

"I think I might have access to that fly," she began. "I mean, I know someone. Maybe he can tell us more."

It took a bit more digging–her purse was definitely in need of a purging–but Leah finally found what she'd been looking for: the business card given to her by Detective Mark Albertson. She held up the card to Gloria.

"This is the detective who interviewed me about finding

Hatchet's body," she said as Gloria took the card from her. "The second detective, that is. He seemed very approachable and nice, much more so than the first detective I talked with."

Gloria studied the card carefully. "So, you could just call him?" she asked, a strong hint of skepticism in her voice. "And he'll, like, tell you stuff?"

Leah shrugged. "It can't hurt to ask," she said. "Plus, I sort of got the sense that he liked me. Sort of. Maybe. I don't know."

"Nice," Gloria said with a wicked grin. "Well, if you can get answers from him on what the police think they have on Claudia, that would be fantastic." She took another long sip of her wine. "After that, you'll have to ask him to turn his deductive powers to help figure out why Dylan has shown up out of the blue."

Leah had briefly forgotten about the sudden and surprising appearance of her ex-boyfriend. She shuddered involuntarily as she flashed back to seeing him in the front row during the show.

"I can't believe I just looked down and saw him there," she said, shaking her head at the memory. "I'm amazed I was able to go on."

"Hey, by the way, great job tonight," Gloria said, leaning forward to clink glasses with her friend. "With all the hullabaloo, I haven't had the chance to properly congratulate you on what was, without question, one hell of an achievement."

They clinked their respective glasses and Gloria smiled at Leah. "I got the sense that you wanted to kill me in that Board meeting this morning," she said with a wide grin. "When I offered you up as our home-grown Aunt Abby understudy."

"What makes you think I still don't want to kill you?" Leah said as she turned on her best Cheshire Cat smile. "Did you happen to notice a slight whiff of elderberry in your wine?"

Gloria glanced down at the glass and then up at Leah. "Come on, admit it: You had a blast tonight."

Leah shrugged. "I will confess there were moments of fun in the midst of the madness," she said slowly. "But to be honest, I couldn't have done it without Alex."

"Which one was Alex? Tell me he was that young, juicy cop."

"No, Alex plays Dr. Einstein," Leah said as she looked around the room, ignoring her lusty friend's comment.

She had spotted many of the cast members when she and Gloria had come in, with one group seated at a large table by the window and another nestled in a corner. She hadn't recognized it before, but looking at the tables from this perspective, she realized the two groups were divided almost entirely by age–the under-thirty crowd at one table and the older thespians at another.

Alex was seated at the table with the older actors, clearly listening patiently to one of Stuart Wilde's long jokes or endless limericks. He glanced over and noticed that both Leah and her friend were looking at him.

Seeing that she'd been caught, Leah gave him a quick wave and then held up her glass, as if toasting him from across the room. Using this sudden attention as a justification to escape, Alex excused himself, grabbed his drink and started to make his way to their table.

"That's him," Leah said, turning to Gloria. "That's Alex."

"He's cute," Gloria said as they watched him wend his way through the crowded bar. "Not cute like that hot, young cop actor, but cute. Of course, he's too age-appropriate for my tastes, but he's a perfectly suitable candidate for you."

"Knock it off," Leah said through clenched teeth. "Don't start playing matchmaker with me. Not tonight."

"Wait," Gloria said as Alex got closer. "I've seen him before, in other shows. He's a terrific actor. I didn't recognize him under that wig and mustache."

Before Leah could respond, Alex arrived at their table.

"Thanks for saving me from another one of Stuart's limericks," Alex said. "It was an epic one, with multiple stanzas, covering many generations and several far-flung locations. Those poor folks could be there for days."

"I didn't actually intend to drag you over," Leah admitted as she gestured to one of the empty chairs. "I was just explaining to

Gloria how you saved me today. I couldn't have done it without you."

Alex swatted the compliment away with his hand. "You had all the words, you just needed some help bringing them back," he said, and then turned to Gloria and extended his hand. "I'm Alex, by the way."

"Oh, I'm familiar with your work," Gloria said. From where Leah sat, it looked like her friend was almost blushing.

"Gloria is on the theater's Board," Leah said by way of explanation. "President of the Board, actually. She's the reason I was offered the Executive Director job."

"Thank you for that," Alex said.

"Well, don't be so quick with your thanks. She's also the reason I've ended up playing Aunt Abby," Leah added sarcastically, with a sidelong glance at Gloria. But her friend wasn't taking the bait and was still looking intently at Alex.

"I saw you in *A View From the Bridge*, as Eddie," Gloria said, sounding uncharacteristically breathless. "Just wonderful, amazing. And then, like the very next show, you were insanely funny. *Room Service*, right?"

"Yep, Leo Davis from Oswego," Alex said.

"And then, like a month later, *Travesties*, with that incredibly long opening monologue," Gloria said.

"Henry Carr, of the Consulate," Alex intoned, and then quickly slipped into a perfect British accent. *"'He was Irish, of course...,'"* he began and then broke into a grin. "Don't get me started on that one, we'll be here all night. *'Do it on my head, caviar for the general public.'"*

"You're a really good actor," Gloria said.

"Thank you."

"I keep telling him that," Leah said in agreement.

"I mean, I work at a big theater, you may have heard of it," Gloria continued. "We're right across the river. And over there we have lots of so-called professional actors. So believe me when I tell you, you are a <u>really</u> good actor."

"Thank you," Alex repeated, looking a bit embarrassed at this sudden and effusive praise.

"Are those two tables really separated by age," Leah said, in an attempt to change the subject. "Or is that just a trick of the light?"

Alex glanced back at his actor friends and their odd, age-driven segregation.

"No, you nailed it," he said. "For some reason, they self-select by age when it comes to post-show drinks. I divide my time pretty evenly between the two tables. I'm subtly working on bringing both sides to some sort of Armistice."

"What tactics are you using?" Leah asked.

"Oh, something along the lines of, 'Hey, why don't we all stop dividing by age and sit at one table?'" Alex said with a laugh. "I mean, they're actors. No point in wasting time on subtlety."

This produced a hearty laugh from the two women, which was suddenly cut short when Gloria glanced behind Leah. Her eyes went a little wide.

"Good evening," came a too-familiar voice. Leah's own laugh stuck in her throat as she turned to see that Dylan was standing there.

"Dylan," she said, her voice coming out in an unexpected rasp.

"In the flesh," he said, flashing his patented smile. Braces in his twenties had clearly been worth the investment; his smile was a walking teeth brightener commercial.

"What are you doing here?" Despite her best effort, Leah's question came out with a little sputtering and stammering.

"Oh, just passing through the Midwest on a bit of a road trip, doing the Kerouac thing," he said. "A Gonzo-style adventure before settling into a gig at a theater out West. *Zen and the Art of the Ford Fiesta*, you know, the whole deal." He glanced across the table. "Gloria, good to see you again."

"Dylan," she said flatly.

"Effusive as ever," he said with a grin. He turned to Alex and put out his hand. "I'm Dylan, by the way."

"Alex," he replied, looking from Leah to Gloria for direction before shaking Dylan's hand in the most perfunctory way he could manage.

"Alex is Leah's boyfriend," Gloria said suddenly. Both Leah and Alex turned to her, surprised by this announcement.

"Fantastic," Dylan said as he pulled over an unused chair from a nearby table. He was already slouching before his butt had hit the seat. "And what do you do, Alex?"

"I'm—" he began, but Gloria cut him off.

"He's an actor," she said, declaring it with great finality.

"Lovely. Anything I might have seen you in?" Dylan asked as he waved at a passing waitress.

"Well, I'm not sure—" Alex began, but again Gloria cut him off.

"He's a mainstay at the theater I work at," Gloria said. "You know, the big one across the river. You auditioned for us once there, didn't you Dylan? How did that go?"

"There was nothing suitable for me at the time," he said, the ice audible in his tone.

"Three stages, twenty-five to thirty productions a year, and *nothing* for a white male in his early thirties?" Gloria said with a slow shake of her head, her voice dripping with sarcasm. "What are the odds?"

Dylan ignored her question and kept his attention focused on Alex. "You in anything right now?" he asked. Dylan's tone and manner were casual, but this attitude was betrayed by the intensity in his eyes.

Before Alex could generate an answer, Gloria once again jumped in.

"*Krapp's Last Tape,*" she said quickly. "You know, Samuel Becket. And *The Diary of a Madman,*" she added, wanting to add a quick, impressive boost to this spur-of-the-moment fictional resumé.

"In rep?" Dylan asked, the surprise evident in his voice.

"No, better than that, an evening of one acts," Gloria said as she turned to Alex for unneeded confirmation. Alex nodded along anyway and then looked to Leah. After a long moment, she nodded in agreement.

"Yes, both plays, back-to-back," Alex said. "With a quick set change, of course."

"Of course," Dylan agreed. *"Krapp's Last Tape* and *The Diary of a Madman*? That's a lot to tackle. In one night."

"He's brilliant," Gloria stated. "Isn't he, Leah?" She gave her friend a long, penetrating look.

"He sure is," Leah said as she reached over and clasped Alex's hand. "Alex is a fantastic actor."

She and Alex locked eyes for a second and she could see that he completely understood the situation. And he was also clearly enjoying the twist it had taken.

"Oh, hon, you're embarrassing me," Alex said with mock humility. He leaned over and gave Leah a quick kiss on the cheek. "You're going to give me a big head with all this talk."

Alex then turned to Dylan, who had observed the brief kiss with great interest.

"So, Dylan, which theater are you headed to out West?" he said as he readjusted his loving grasp of Leah's outstretched hand. "Berkeley Rep? The Geffen? La Jolla Playhouse?"

Dylan shook his head.

"The Old Globe in San Diego?" Alex continued. "Pasadena Playhouse? ACT in Seattle? Southcoast Repertory? Laguna Playhouse? American Conservatory Theater in San Francisco?"

Alex rattled the list off so quickly, Leah had difficulty keeping up with him. Dylan, however, had no such trouble.

"None of those," he said slowly, much of the flippancy gone from his voice.

"Some other theater, then," Alex said.

"Yes," Dylan finally replied.

Leah watched the two men staring each other down. The moment seemed to be awkward for Dylan. However, if his expression was any indication, Alex was having an absolute blast.

"Which theater is it?" Alex finally asked, his tone as casual as could be. "Have I heard of it?"

"The Bakersfield Playhouse," Dylan said.

"Oh. You mean the one in Bakersfield?" Alex asked.

"That's the one," Dylan said. He was clearly not happy with how this encounter was unfolding.

"That's a long way to go, hope it's a great part," Alex said. Although Alex hadn't framed his remark as a question, it obviously was intended as one. Finally Dylan couldn't ignore the pressure any longer.

"I'll be playing various roles," he said flatly.

"Variety. You gotta love it," Alex said.

Dylan turned to Leah. "I was hoping you and I could have a chance to talk. While I'm in town," he said. "Clear the air and all."

"This is Minnesota," Leah said. "The air is already plenty clear."

"I don't think we left things at a good place back in New York," he continued, lowering his voice and–with his body language–trying to give the impression they were the only two people at the table.

Unfortunately for him, they weren't.

"Dylan, I can't speak for Leah," Gloria said. "But we're having a nice time here and you weren't invited to this party."

The waitress Dylan had waved at earlier arrived at the table, pad in hand, but Gloria gestured her away.

"He's not staying," Gloria said.

Dylan looked up at the waitress. "Looks like I'm not staying," he said as he pushed his chair back from the table and gave her his brightest smile. "But thanks for coming over." For some reason, he felt the need to end this statement with a wink at the young server.

The waitress was too busy to give the situation anything

more than a quick glance. She moved on to another group, a rowdy bunch of frat boys, who were waving her down.

Dylan stood up and looked at Leah. He was giving her his best repentant puppy dog look.

"Anyway, I'd love to talk if you have some time in the next few days. My number hasn't changed," he added.

"Mine has," Leah said.

"I know. You're a tough lady to track down."

"That's by design." Leah looked up at him. "Dylan, I've got a pretty busy next few days, but I'll see what I can do."

"Thanks," he said. "I appreciate it." He turned to the others at the table. "Alex, nice to meet you. Gloria."

He gave her a quick nod and moved into the crowd, headed toward the door.

Leah didn't turn to watch him go, but instead looked over at Gloria. "Thanks for that," she said. "Thanks for the save."

Gloria held up her hand. "The exit is not yet complete," she said, watching as Dylan made his way across the room. "Does he turn and give you one last mournful look before leaving the stage?"

She continued to observe, while both Leah and Alex worked hard not to follow her gaze.

Dylan pushed the door open and–before stepping out into the night–he turned and looked longingly back toward Leah.

"Bingo," Gloria said, slapping her hand on the table. "A slow turn, a sad look, the head droops and Mr. Dylan disappears into the darkness. All right on cue."

"Thanks for stepping in there," Leah said as she turned to Alex. "As I'm guessing you've already figured out, that was my old boyfriend."

"Nice improv skills," Gloria added.

"Thanks. I took two years of training at Dudley Riggs' Brave New Workshop, back in the day," Alex said. He had relaxed into his chair and took a big sip from his drink. "That was fun. I could have done it all night long."

"Thankfully, that wasn't required," Leah said. "But I think

you did it long enough–and well enough–to shut him down. At least for the time being."

"Now I'm just dying to know what roles he'll be playing at the Bakersfield Playhouse," Alex said.

"I'd be surprised if it were anything more significant than Spear Carrier #3," Gloria said with a laugh. "What a putz–sorry, Leah, but he's a putz."

"No offense taken," Leah said. "No one is more aware of that than I. But enough of that jerk." She turned to Alex. "So you're doing both "*Krapp's Last Tape* and *The Diary of a Madman*? That's a lot to tackle. In one night."

Leah captured Dylan's inflections with a mimic's skill.

"Yes, it's quite the artistic challenge," Alex replied, slipping easily into his officious actor character. "It is perhaps my toughest role since playing Maggie in *Cat on a Hot Tin Roof*."

"That was an all-puppet cast, wasn't it?" Leah asked, as the emotional stench from Dylan's visit started to lift. "Marionettes, am I right?"

"Yes, frightfully difficult to maneuver," Alex continued. "One night my strings got entangled with Big Daddy's and we had a devil of a time sorting it out."

They continued like this, laughing and joking, until near closing time. She and Gloria and Alex had so much fun that, for a while at least, she forgot about the dead theater critic. And the hospitalized actress. And the Board member who had been taken in for questioning.

It wasn't until she got home and thought to check her phone for messages that she realized she had missed an important call.

It was from Detective Albertson.

He was wondering if she had time to talk to him about the case.

CHAPTER FOURTEEN

"Technically, this is not an official brunch."

Detective Albertson held up his hand, to signal that he needed to clarify his last statement. "That is to say, this is brunch, but this is not an official meeting on the case. Just to be clear."

"Understood," Leah said as she cut another sinfully rich forkful of Eggs Benedict and directed it toward her mouth. "Officially, it's brunch, but that's the only official thing about it."

"Right," Albertson said, as he spread some thick strawberry jam on a slice of wheat toast. They ate in silence for a few blissful moments.

Upon receiving his phone message the night before, Leah had realized it was too late to call him back. So she waited until 9:01 on Sunday morning to return his call.

"Thanks for calling back," he had said when he answered, sounding a little out of breath. "I just wanted to ask you a few questions about the latest developments in the case. But I hate to bother you on a Sunday."

"That's no problem," Leah said. "I have nothing until this afternoon's matinee."

"Well, the thing is, I was just heading out to grab some breakfast," he said. "Care to join me?"

Leah answered in the affirmative and forty-five minutes later she found herself at the Grand Cafe, seated across from Detective Mark Albertson as they both dug into a large and tasty brunch spread.

To Leah, it seemed like the only thing she had said "no" to on the large and tempting menu was a Mimosa. And she only did that because she still needed to perform *Arsenic and Old Lace* in about three hours.

"A better, more mature person would be at home right now, going over my lines again," she said as the waitress topped off her coffee. Leah added some cream and quickly turned the dark brown liquid milky gray.

"I heard you did a great job last night," Albertson said.

"Who told you that?"

He shrugged. "Word gets around." He added more jam to a second slice of toast. "Anyway, as I said, this isn't an official interview. I'm just curious to get your perceptions on the latest developments in the case."

"So you can't tell me anything about the interview last night with Claudia Moffatt?"

He shook his head. "I can neither confirm nor deny," he said.

"Well, you're no fun."

"When it comes to murder investigations, probably not," he agreed. "But, seriously, I would love to get your thoughts on the case."

Leah was surprised at this, as his request seemed genuine.

"Really? Why?"

He shrugged. "Experience has taught me that people on the fringes of an investigation can often provide insight we can't glean from within the eye of the storm."

"Well, I'm not sure what I can offer that you don't already know," Leah began. "I mean, despite the fact that I did play Nancy Drew in a middle school production, I think your deductive skills probably outshine mine."

"If you played Nancy Drew, then you have more training

than most," he said with a smile. "But, seriously, what are your thoughts?"

Leah considered this for a long moment.

"Well," she began. "Plenty of people really disliked Ronald Hatchet, based on how nasty his reviews were. But who might have hated him enough to kill him? I'm sure that's a much smaller pool of suspects."

"One would hope."

"But then to kill him at the theater, or at the very least, leave the body on the stage," Leah continued. "That doesn't seem very random. It's like there's a message behind that choice, we just don't fully understand what it means."

"Not yet."

Leah nodded. "Plus, so many people have access to the theater and the stage."

"That does make it more difficult," Albertson agreed.

"The new security cameras will be going in tomorrow," Leah continued. "So from now on we'll have a record of who is coming and going. But that doesn't really help in regards to the death of Ronald Hatchet, does it?"

"Not really," Albertson said. "And then, what about Joan O'Malley, the actress who fell down the stairs?"

"Or was she pushed?" Leah added.

"She says she was," Albertson said.

"But she has a history of exaggeration and outright lying," Leah said.

"Allegedly."

"Allegedly," Leah repeated. "Yeah, I don't know about her and that story. Sure, she's a miserable person, but is that enough reason to shove her down the stairs?"

"It might be for someone," he said.

"And then there's Claudia Moffatt, who had at one time a brief affair with Ronald Hatchet. Allegedly," Leah added for good measure.

Detective Albertson raised an eyebrow at this revelation. "And where did you learn this alleged fact?"

"Word gets around," Leah said, suppressing a smile. "And there is–to some people–the belief that Hatchet's reviews actually got nicer, at least for a bit, while they were an alleged item."

"That is something which would be fairly easy to verify," Albertson said, setting down his fork and taking a small notepad from his sport coat pocket. He quickly scribbled a couple words and then slid the pad back into the coat.

"Unofficial notes?" Leah said with a smile.

"Completely," he said.

A thought occurred to Leah. "You know, speaking of Hatchet's reviews, it occurred to me that the only person who he seemed to have liked in *Arsenic and Old Lace* was Joan O'Malley. He raved about her and then trashed the rest of the cast."

"So he finally wrote something positive about the theater," Albertson offered.

"Yes, but he trashed the rest of the show so thoroughly, that praising one actor doesn't really help the show.

"And yet," she continued, thinking back to the bulletin board, "Someone went to the trouble to post a copy of that review in the dressing room."

"And that's odd?"

Leah shrugged. "Well, it's the theater, so the bar for odd is set pretty low. But, yes, it is strange to post such a negative review in a place where everyone would continually see it and be reminded of it."

Leah stirred her coffee absently while she thought about this some more. "In reality, there is only one person who would benefit from posting that review, and that would be Joan O'Malley. You know, just to rub everyone's nose in it."

"Is that the sort of thing she would be likely to do?"

"I don't know," Leah said as she lifted her cup and took a sip. "I only met her briefly. But based on what everyone has said about her, I wouldn't put it past her."

"It's a pretty thoughtless thing to do," Albertson said.

"Or very thoughtful," Leah added. "But not in a nice way. Flat out annoying, really."

Albertson nodded. "But the question is: Was it annoying enough to drive someone to push her down a flight of stairs?"

"I don't know," Leah said as she set her coffee cup down. "But as alleged questions go, that's an excellent one."

* * *

Leah took another quick look at the get-well card for Joan O'Malley tacked on the bulletin board as she headed toward the makeup table to get ready for that afternoon's matinee.

Two signatures had been added to the card since she had written her brief statement. One was from young Monica, who included a large smiley face with her message, although Leah couldn't quite make out the words in the scrawled missive. The other note was from Doris. It said simply, "Aunt Martha misses Aunt Abby. Please come back to us soon!"

"That was a nice sentiment you wrote on Joan's card," Leah said as she settled into her chair in front of the makeup mirror. Doris was already in place and was toiling away at applying red to her cheeks.

"Thank you, dear," Doris said, and then turned and lowered her voice. "Although, to be honest, it wasn't truly from the heart. If I had my way, you'd finish out the run."

"Well, thank you," Leah said as she began to unscrew the tops off of the small jars in front of her. "My mindset is, I'm just doing this one show at a time. I'll be happy to get today's matinee behind me and then we can start to worry about next weekend."

"And of course tomorrow night's Pay What You Can show," Doris added.

Leah had forgotten about the additional Monday night performance. She sighed deeply. "Yes, of course, we can't forget tomorrow night."

"You did so well last night," Doris continued. "Really remarkable."

"I couldn't have done it without you," Leah said. "You saved my butt about a dozen times."

"No problem," Doris said. "I learned early on in rehearsal that Joan wasn't always going to be one hundred percent on her lines. So I just memorized both characters."

"That's a lot of work."

"It actually made it easier," Doris said. "Helped me get back in the swing, not having done a play for so long."

"How long have you been away from the stage?" Leah looked over at the older woman, who was studying her face in the mirror.

"Oh, goodness, years and years and years," Doris said with a little laugh. "Too many to count. What with raising a family and then spending the last few years dealing with health issues as a caregiver, the time just sort of slipped away. You know, the way it does."

She turned to Leah. "I lost my husband, my beloved Al, two years ago, which left me dealing with everything all on my own. But after a while I finally just thought, 'What the heck!,' and went back out on auditions. It took a while to get into the swing of things, but here I am. And I'm loving it! It's like I never left."

The older woman's joy was practically infectious and Leah couldn't help smile along with her.

"What was your last role before playing Aunt Martha?" Leah asked, turning away from her makeup work.

"Let me think,' Doris said as she set down a small brush. "That's a lot of years ago. It would have to be Prudence in *Beyond Therapy*, I think. By Christopher Durang. Do you know it?"

"I know it well," Leah said, breaking into a wide smile. "I did it in summer stock and had hoped to stage it again at the little theater I had in New York. What was your favorite role?"

"Well, of course at the time I was the right age for a lot of ingénues, but one time I was lucky enough to get the part of Tracy Lord."

"*The Philadelphia Story*," Leah said.

"*The Philadelphia Story* indeed! I think I was only cast because at the time I had red hair. Naturally red hair," Doris added with a grin. "But, all in all, I think I did the part justice."

"I'm sure you did," Leah agreed. "So, now that you're back in the swing of things, will we see more of you around here?"

"Well, I certainly hope so. I guess it all comes down to being cast, doesn't it?"

"Yes, there is always that," Leah agreed as she turned back to her mirror. "Here's a word to the wise: We've got *The Importance of Being Earnest* coming up soon."

"Lady Bracknell," Doris said, smiling warmly at the mention of the name. "Goodness, I'm finally old enough to play Lady Bracknell." She switched into a flawless English accent. "'*To lose one parent, Mr. Worthing, may be regarded as a misfortune; to lose both looks like carelessness.*'"

"You've got to audition for that role," Leah said, laughing at the famous line. "You'd be fantastic."

"Thank you, dear," Doris said as she smiled at the prospect.

"Well," Leah said as she reached for an eyebrow pencil. "I hope a little of last night's terror has worn off, so I can have at least a bit of fun out there this afternoon."

"That's the spirit," Doris said as she stood up and pulled her costume from the rack. "And not to worry, I'll be right there to catch you. If you need me."

Costume in hand, she headed toward the privacy of the women's changing room and Leah returned her attention to the process of aging herself. She gave herself a long look in the mirror, convinced that the previous twenty-four hours had conveniently added several new lines to her face.

"Fifteen minutes," Kanisha shouted as she sailed through the room.

"Thank you, fifteen," Leah said in semi-unison with the other actors.

"And while I have your attention," Kanisha continued, her tone suggesting a group admonishment was pending, "I've said it before and I don't feel I need to say it again: Stop snacking on the prop food in the kitchen. It's clearly labeled."

Leah looked up at her. "Are we okay for this afternoon's show?"

The Stage Manager shrugged. "We'll get by. You'll just have to serve smaller slices of cake to Officers Brophy and Klein. And I'll have to get more grape juice before tomorrow night's show to replace some missing elderberry wine."

"Someone must be mighty thirsty to risk taking a swig of the elderberry wine," Leah mused.

"Actors," Kanisha replied, and then she swept out of the room and onto her other long list of pre-show duties.

"Actors indeed," Leah muttered quietly and then she turned her attention back to finishing her make-up.

* * *

Leah made her way through the dimly lit backstage area, script in hand, headed toward her entrance point for the top of the show. Alex, who wasn't on for most of Act One, was already there, peering through a small opening in the set, looking out at the audience.

"How does the house look?" Leah asked as she set her script down on the rickety table near her primary entrance and exit point–the kitchen of the Brewster house. Even backstage she got this door turned around with the one that supposedly led to the Brewster's cellar. So the small table had become a helpful directional beacon for her.

"Old," Alex whispered in response to her question. "They look very old. And the few younger faces I can see really accentuate how old the rest of the audience is."

"Well, perhaps you'd like to join the theater's committee dedicated to growing a more youthful audience to help build our future," Leah suggested. "It's the Grab Our Youth committee."

Alex turned sharply from his audience gazing. "You actually

have a committee called Grab Our Youth? Are you insane? That's going to get you all brought up on charges."

Leah looked up from her script and grinned at him. "Gotcha!," she said.

Alex shook his head, ashamed he had been so easily fooled. "Well, given all the committees this theater has, it wouldn't surprise me if they'd come up with something like that. Every time you look around here, there's another committee doing something. I'm surprised you don't have a Committee on Committees, just to oversee all the groups."

Leah was about to point out that was essentially the purpose of the Board, but before she could say anything, Alex was headed toward the stairs to the dressing rooms to finish his makeup.

"Have a great show," he murmured as he smoothly slipped past her.

"You too," Leah whispered in response. "Oh, and that was fun last night."

Alex turned and smiled at her. "Yes, it was," he said, and then he disappeared into the backstage darkness.

There was the sound of applause from the other side of the set and Leah could hear Gloria, who was the Board Member on Duty for this matinee, as she went through the standard welcome speech.

Leah flipped the pages of her script to the beginning and did a quick review of her first lines. Then she flipped ahead to a problem section about five minutes in. She was still reviewing those troublesome lines when Gloria got to the part in her speech about "turning off your cell phones for the duration of the show."

Gloria's presentation was charming if straightforward; she didn't go in for the jokes that Gavin and some of the other Board members preferred. She just wanted to, as she put it, "tell them what I need to tell them and then get the hell off the stage."

The mention of cell phones reminded Leah that she had

slipped her own phone into her Aunt Abby apron, intending to set it next to her script on her wobbly table.

As she pulled it out and examined it–to ensure it was actually set on silent–she noticed that she had received a text at some point in the last couple of hours.

The sender was UNKNOWN and the message was short and sweet.

It read: *"Stop doing this play. Or you are going to die."*

CHAPTER FIFTEEN

Somehow–she wasn't sure how–Leah made it through Act One.

A numbness settled in after reading the threatening text on her phone, but before she could process its meaning any further, there was a whispered call for "Places." Moments later, Leah found herself on the dark stage, waiting for the lights to come on and hoping in her heart that they never would.

But of course they did and it then fell to Leah to kick off the play with its first line, a gentle compliment to the kindly old Rev. Dr. Harper, who looked over his glasses at her as she held a small teapot in her trembling hand. She wasn't sure where the quivering was coming from–common stage fright or intense fear for her life–but regardless of its source, she knew she had to start the show. She smiled at the two actors sharing the stage with her and they smiled back, little sparks of desperation starting to appear behind their eyes.

And then the line came.

"*'Yes, indeed, my sister Martha and I have been talking all week about your sermon last Sunday,'*" Leah said, gathering speed. "*'It's really wonderful, Dr. Harper—in only two short years you've taken on the spirit of Brooklyn.'*"

That was all it took to put her back on track. Her character was supposed to be distracted and a little off and Leah was certain those attributes were coming across loud and clear in her performance.

Things began to go a little smoother once Doris arrived as Aunt Martha, and then when Alex appeared as Dr. Einstein, she felt like she could almost relax.

Almost.

Any attempt to not think about the text only made her think about it even more, which completely got in the way of her being able to do anything else–like recite lines and act, the very things she was on stage to do.

Finally, mercifully, the end of the act came. Leah rushed back to her phone, hoping against hope she had simply misread an otherwise benign message.

One look at her phone told her otherwise. The message was still there: *"Stop doing this play. Or you are going to die."*

With a mere fifteen minutes before she was due back on stage, Leah made two very quick phone calls.

* * *

"We can run a trace on the phone number, but I suspect the message came from a burner," Detective Albertson said as he looked down at Leah's phone cupped in his hand. "Which means the trace will lead us nowhere. But we should at least start there."

Albertson sat across the Board Room table from Leah and Gloria. The play had ended uneventfully–if you didn't count yet another enthusiastic standing ovation, which she actually found annoying because it meant she had to spend even more time on stage.

Leah had learned years before that a Minnesota standing ovation was as commonplace as mosquitos in summer. Minnesota audiences were often so thrilled the performers had made it safely to the end of a performance, they felt the only proper reward was to greet that arrival with a standing ovation.

From a grade school variety show to Pavarotti, everyone received the same, occasionally undeserved ovation.

"So there's no way to find out who the text came from?" Gloria said, her intense annoyance at technology clear in her voice.

"Probably not," Detective Albertson said. "With the help of the service provider, we might be able to run a triangulation, which won't tell us who made the call, but will at least give us an idea of where it came from. And that could be helpful."

He turned from Gloria to Leah.

"Of course, my recommendation to you is that you withdraw from the play. Immediately," he added. "If I'm reading your schedule properly, the theater has five days to find and train a replacement; there may even be someone within the cast who can step in. But regardless, I think we need to take this threat seriously."

"I do take it seriously," Leah said. She was still dressed in her Aunt Abby costume, her face still covered in the old-age makeup she had so carefully applied. "But I have an obligation to the theater. And we don't have five days, because we have a Pay What You Can performance tomorrow night." She turned to Gloria for support. "What do you think I should do?"

"I don't know, hon," Gloria said slowly. "It is only a play, after all."

"A play that's giving the theater a tremendous financial boost," Leah said. "A boost we really need."

"I can't argue with that," Gloria agreed. "Although I really wish I could."

Leah turned back to Albertson across the table. "And if we shut down the play, what then? What does that do to your chances of finding whoever killed Ronald Hatchet? Or whoever pushed Joan O'Malley?"

"If she was indeed pushed," Albertson added, his tone tentative.

"Whatever," Leah said. "Look, I was browbeaten by an idiot boyfriend in New York for five years and I did nothing about it.

I'm tired of being a doormat. That ends now." She stood up and walked toward the door to the small room.

"I'm not letting some anonymous troll shut down a successful show with a vague threat because he–or she–is carrying a grudge or doesn't like the play or whatever their idiotic issue might be," Leah continued. "As trite as it sounds, the show must go on." She walked out the door.

After a long moment, Gloria turned to Detective Albertson. "I can't believe she exited on that line."

Before he could respond, Leah was back in the doorway.

"Can we all pretend I didn't say that last thing," she said quietly. "If anyone asks, I just stormed out and never said 'the show must go on.' Okay?"

"Sure thing," Gloria said. Detective Albertson nodded in agreement as Leah headed downstairs to peel off her makeup.

* * *

Detective Albertson offered to drive Leah home, but she declined. They were standing by the front door to the theater. The lobby was empty and it looked like the last of the actors had taken off.

"Gloria's already made an offer and, anyway, I feel like I've taken up enough of your time today," Leah said.

"Well, that's not true, but okay. Be careful. And be alert," he said firmly as he turned to go. "And don't be afraid to call me."

"That's nice, but I can't," she said.

"Yes you can. Any time. Day or night."

"No, I can't because you've got my cell," she said, pointing at the phone in his hand. "You were going to trace or triangulate or something with it."

"Oh, sorry, we don't need to keep your phone for that," he said. "I have your number and your cell provider, that's all we require at this point. They'll have all the information we need to go on."

He handed the phone back to her.

"But, seriously," he said. "Call me if anything happens. Call before it happens."

"That would be a good trick."

"You know what I mean."

Leah nodded. "I do and I will," she said with a quick smile. "And thanks for brunch today."

"Unofficial brunch," he replied. "Thanks for joining me."

He pushed open the door, revealing that–despite Leah having performed an entire full-length show, plus taken part in a short police investigation–the sun was still out. Blindingly so. She squinted at it as the door swung shut.

"You know, you could have blown me off and let him drive you home," Gloria said. She was at the far end of the lobby and had apparently heard at least the last part of their conversation. "Or are you playing hard to get?"

"The only person I'm playing hard to get with is that nut bar who sent that text message," Leah said. "Let's get out of here. I've had enough of this place for one day."

* * *

"You know, on second thought, I really could have driven myself home," Leah said once they were in Gloria's Miata and on their way. Gloria had pealed out of the theater's parking lot at a high speed, spraying gravel as she did. And Leah wasn't entirely certain there actually was any gravel in that lot.

"Sure, that's just what the nut bar was expecting you to do," Gloria said as she sailed through a yield sign. "I think for the next couple days, you need to lay low. And not driving your own car is a good first step in that direction."

"Sure, but then how do I get back to the theater tomorrow? My car's still in the lot."

"Take a cab," Gloria said, touching the brakes lightly as she glided through a four-way stop. "The theater will reimburse you."

"Do you have the power to approve an expenditure such as that? It could be as much as $15."

"Hey, I'm the president of the Board of Directors. I can spend up to $75 without getting Board approval," she replied.

"Just don't let that power go to your head," Leah said as she surreptitiously clutched at the passenger door handle while Gloria maneuvered around a tight turn. She considered for a moment that she might be in far more danger riding with Gloria than she was continuing in *Arsenic and Old Lace*.

* * *

It was a short, but heart attack-inducing drive. In about half the time it took Leah to drive the same route, Gloria brought her car to a screeching stop in front of Leah's condo building. Leah caught her breath and then began to dig through her purse for her keys.

"What do you want to do about the show tomorrow night?" Gloria asked.

"Perform it," Leah said without looking up from her search.

"There's no reason why we can't call it off," Gloria began, but Leah held up her hand, in which she was now holding her keys.

"It will be a big money-maker for the theater, and it's a chance for other theater folks in town who are busy with their own shows to come see it. That's good PR for us," Leah said as she sorted through the small cluster of keys. "Plus, Detective Albertson said they would have plainclothes officers in and around the theater. So what's the worst thing that could happen?"

"I don't even want to think about the worst thing that could happen."

"You and me both," Leah said, leaning over and giving Gloria a quick kiss on the cheek. "See you tomorrow."

Gloria waited to make sure Leah made it safely into the building before pulling away, cutting into traffic without signaling and then waving happily to the drivers who honked at her.

Leah stopped in the lobby to check for mail. It wasn't until she'd gotten her mailbox open and saw it was nearly empty that she realized it was Sunday. The contents consisted of a notice from the condo board about repainting the parking stripes in the garage. She locked the box and moved to the elevator, pressing the button while she jammed the notice into her purse.

The elevator was empty and the ride was quick. Once she'd reached her floor, she realized she had put her keys back in her purse, which then required another plunge into that mess to retrieve them so she could get into her apartment.

She was doing just that when she heard a voice. She looked up from her purse dive.

"Leah."

Dylan was standing next to her apartment door. The hallway light was above and behind him, which threw his face into shadow. But she immediately recognized the voice and the slouching silhouette as belonging to her persistent ex-boyfriend.

"How did you find out where I live?" Leah said sharply.

Dylan shrugged, pushing the boyish charm thing to its limits. "I'm ashamed to say that I followed you home last night," he said.

"Well, that's not creepy, is it? And how did you get into the building?" Leah's tone was an even mixture of anger and annoyance.

"Charm, mostly," he said. "Hold a door for someone who's arms are full and they forget to check if you belong here or not."

"Well, you don't belong here," Leah said. She considered whether she was better off heading back to the lobby or going into her apartment. Either choice had its pluses and minuses.

"I only want to have a short conversation with you," he said, using his soft, thoughtful voice. Leah's stomach turned at the sound.

"I've had more than enough conversations with you, Dylan. Enough to last a lifetime."

She decided it was better to forge ahead and get herself into her apartment, so she moved toward the deadbolt, the key extended from her fist like a shiv. She unlocked the door and swung it open in one smooth action, stepping into her apartment. She turned quickly, to keep the door between her and Dylan.

"I want you to leave now so I don't have to go to the trouble of throwing you out later."

"Can we just talk?"

"You have thirty seconds. Go," Leah said flatly.

Dylan sighed and shook his head. "I came here to ask you to come back. To me. And to the theater. To our theater. The one we built together," he said, his eyes avoiding hers. "I came to say I'm sorry and to ask you to forgive me."

"Not going to happen. You have five more seconds."

"I came to tell you that I love you."

"Time's up. Good night." Leah shut the door and flipped the deadbolt, then added the chain for good measure. She leaned against the door for a long moment, trying to steady her breath.

She listened closely. There was no sound coming from the hall. She turned, quietly, and peered through the peephole in the center of the door. Its fisheye lens gave her a wide view of the hallway. Dylan appeared to be gone.

Leah fought the temptation to swing the door open and check both ends of the hall, just to be sure that he had in fact departed. Instead, she walked calmly into her kitchen, took a mug from the cabinet and began to boil water for tea.

She realized that her heart was beating extra fast and she wasn't sure if she'd actually taken a breath in the last two minutes. She sat down on a chair and leaned forward, resting her forehead on the palms of her hands. After a few moments, she heard soft moaning. It took a second for her to realize that the sound was coming from her own throat.

She was relaxing into the whimper, letting it morph into a form of meditation to help calm her spirit, when she heard another sound.

It was a weak knock at her door; not even really an official knock. More like a feeble, uninspired tap.

"Dylan, you are, without question, the most annoying person in the history of the world," she mumbled as she got up and headed toward the door. With the chain still in place, she yanked the door open, ready to read him the riot act.

"I told you to go away," she began, and then suddenly stopped. It wasn't Dylan standing in her hallway, trying to puppy dog his way back in.

It was Claudia Moffatt.

And she looked dreadful.

CHAPTER SIXTEEN

Although she might have been embarrassed to admit it, the first thought Leah had when she saw Claudia Moffatt standing in her doorway was, "I need to talk to the Condo Board about the security in this building. It is beyond lax."

The second, more pressing thought was, "Why is Claudia Moffatt standing in my doorway?"

"I'm so sorry to bother you," Claudia said. "I just needed to talk. To someone."

"Sure, no problem, by all means," Leah said quickly. "Just let me get the chain here..." She shut the door and slid the chain off, then opened the door wide to allow the older woman to enter.

Claudia came in, looking a little dazed and more than a little haggard. She was still wearing the matching top and skirt from the night before, but everything was wrinkled and askew. Her mass of hair was also frizzled and cockeyed, while her make-up had smeared and faded.

"I'm so sorry to bother you," Claudia repeated. She looked a bit unsteady on her feet, so Leah extended a hand and took her by the elbow, directing the large woman toward a chair in the living room. Claudia sat heavily, sighing as she sank into the chair.

Once she was sure Claudia was safely seated, Leah headed back to close and lock the door. She again slid the chain in place.

"Do you want some tea?" she asked. "I have water boiling."

"If it's no trouble, tea would be just the thing," Claudia said as she finally began to relax into the chair.

"No problem at all," Leah said as she headed to the kitchen. The water she had put on for her own tea was just beginning to boil. She quickly put together a cup and saucer and then carried the hot liquid back to the living room.

"Given the part I'm currently playing, I'm not sure how wise it is to be accepting a cup of tea from me," Leah joked as she set the cup on the small table next to Claudia's chair.

"Poisoning me would be the kindest thing you can do right now," Claudia replied as she picked up the teacup and took a sip. "Take me right out of my misery." She took another long drink and then set the cup down as she sat back in the chair. She let out another long sigh.

"What a night, what a day," she said. "I suppose you heard the police took me in for questioning?"

Leah nodded.

"Right in the lobby," Claudia continued. "Right in the middle of intermission. No warning, just 'Would you please come along with us, you can call your lawyer from the precinct house.'"

"And did you?"

"Did I what?" Claudia was looking around the small living room. She seemed distant and distracted as she turned back to Leah.

"Did you call your lawyer?"

"You can be assured that I did," Claudia said, a haughty tone now evident in her voice. "And you can be just as sure that it didn't do a whit of good. Not one whit. They questioned me last night, put me in a jail cell of all places, and then questioned me again this morning. The exact same questions, just this time in a different order."

"And your lawyer couldn't do anything?"

Claudia shook her head. "Oh, he was useless. Useless I tell

you. Charges me $450 an hour to tell me the police are well within their rights to hold me for up to 48 hours for questioning, this being a capital crime and all. Then he goes home to his bed in Wayzata and I'm stuck in a cell with the road company of *Chicago*. Outrageous."

Leah waited to make sure Claudia had concluded her rant, because she wanted to ask a question that had been hanging in the air since the night before.

"Do the police really think you had something to do with Ronald Hatchet's death?" she asked, keeping her tone as tentative as possible.

"That would appear to be the case," Claudia said. "Based on their line of questioning."

"What did you tell them?"

Claudia looked over at her, then picked up the cup and finished the tea in one gulp. "I told them what I knew, which is nothing," she said. She gave Leah a long look, clearly trying to come to a decision.

"I'm not sure why I'm here," she finally said. "I know that everyone on the Board hates me, and most were probably delighted to hear I had been hauled in by the police. A dream come true for some, I would imagine."

Leah started to object, but Claudia held up a hand. "Don't bother to deny it. You may be new, but it's got to be clear to even you how the Board feels about me. And, believe me, the feeling is mutual. However, they never had the sense to establish term limits and—in my own way—I love that little theater. So they're stuck with me. For a good long time."

Claudia slowly stood up. Leah began to rise as well, but Claudia gestured that she should stay seated. She began to wander through the living room, examining the three pieces of art Leah had finally gotten around to hanging. She then spent several seconds looking at a ceramic piece on the counter between the living room and the dining area. She picked it up, examined it and then returned it without comment.

"Anyway, I needed to tell someone," Claudia said, turning

back to Leah. "I couldn't tell the Board, so I'm here to tell you what I told the police."

"What did you tell them?"

"That I honestly don't know if I murdered Ronald Hatchet or not."

* * *

"Did you ever meet him? Hatchet?"

Leah shook her head.

Claudia was on her second cup of tea. They had moved from the living room and were seated at the table in the small dining nook, which connected the kitchen to the living room.

Leah had dug through the refrigerator and freezer looking for some form of snack to offer her impromptu guest. She finally located a box of Girl Scout Thin Mint cookies in the back of the small freezer. Leah was surprised to find it there, as she was certain she had polished off all the Girl Scout cookies right after buying them the week she moved in. However, this box had slipped behind a couple bags of frozen vegetables. Once it had been rescued, she and Claudia made quick work of its contents.

"Ronald Hatchet was an odious little man, but he had an undeniable charm, sad to say," Claudia said as she took another of the cold cookies. "Why do the worst men often come across as the most charming? At least, at first."

Leah couldn't help but think of Dylan, who had been the poster boy for charismatic when they had originally met. And then her mind jumped to his recent visit to her home and the sharp change in her feelings toward him.

"I don't know," she said. "Eventually, that fades."

"Indeed it does," Claudia agreed. "Of course, I had met Ronald at the theater, as one does. I'm on the Board, he's a critic, our paths crossed. But then one night we happened to both be dining out, alone.

"I for one," she continued, as her tone shifted, "feel there is no shame in dining alone. Since my divorce from Mr. Moffatt oh those many years ago, I have cultivated the practice and I fully endorse it. As a single woman, I would hope you do the same."

Leah nodded, not sure how the topic had morphed to her relationship status or lack thereof. She didn't have time to consider it as Claudia resumed her story.

"So, we chatted, decided to have dinner together, and then one thing led to another," she said as she thought back on it, her tone now a bit wistful. "For all of his faults, which were legion, Ronald was the rare middle-aged man who held an appreciation for a woman of a certain age."

Claudia took a sip of her tea, reached for a Thin Mint, thought better of it and then decided to go for it anyway. "Our relationship, if you want to call it that, was short but intense. And then one day, he just stopped calling. What's the term? He spirited me?"

"He ghosted you," Leah said.

"Ghosted? Well, that makes just as much sense as spirited," she said with a laugh. "I'm always five years behind on the lingo. LOL, I guess. Anyway, I left him a few messages, which he never returned, and that was that."

"You never saw him again?"

"No, I saw him at the theater a couple of times, but he never approached me and I certainly wasn't going to approach him," she said, starting to sound a little angry at the memory. "I do have my pride, after all."

Claudia took another sip of tea while Leah processed what she'd heard so far. "Based on that, why did the police want to question you about the murder?"

"I believe the path they were headed down was something along the lines of a woman scorned, that sort of thing. You see, they raised the issue of jealousy."

"Jealousy? Of who? Or whom?"

"As part of their investigation, they had discovered that—for a very short amount of time—Ronald Hatchet had written a few *positive* reviews of the theater. Very positive reviews, in fact.

And, as it turned out, the timing of those reviews corresponded to the timeline of our brief affair."

"So the police thought he wrote nice reviews because you two were involved?"

"I believe that was their line of thinking," Claudia said. She took another cookie. "Why are these even more delicious when they're cold? I've never understood that."

"It's a mystery," Leah agreed.

"As part of their investigation," Claudia continued, "they read all of his reviews of the theater's shows and noted that he continued with his savage critiques. Until his most recent review."

"Of *Arsenic and Old Lace*?"

Claudia nodded.

"But he hated that show," Leah said. She remembered how he had lashed out at what she felt were some really fine performances.

"Yes, but he did heap praise on one performer. In stark contrast with the majority of his review."

"Joan O'Malley."

"Exactly. So they asked me if I was aware of any relationship between Joan O'Malley and Ronald Hatchet. Apparently, they had found text messages on his phone that substantiated a recent, ongoing liaison of some kind between the two. Which led them to think someone might be jealous of that association."

"Jealous enough to kill him and then try to kill her, by pushing her down the stairs?"

Claudia nodded. "Apparently," she said. "Farfetched in my mind, yet somehow plausible in theirs."

Leah considered this new information. "So Hatchet was fooling around with Joan O'Malley," she said slowly.

"Like I said, he had an eye for women of a certain age."

"Well, the timing of Hatchet's death is a bit loosey-goosey, but we certainly know the approximate time Joan O'Malley fell —or was pushed—down the stairs. Do you have an alibi for that night?"

Claudia shook her head. "That's where things become difficult," she said, looking down at her teacup to avoid Leah's gaze. "I have little memory of the weekend Ronald Hatchet was killed and no memory of last Friday night at all."

Leah was poised to ask a question, but got the sense that Claudia needed to talk about this at her own pace.

"Since the divorce," she said slowly, "I've gotten into the habit—the bad habit, I am the first to admit—of having a drink or two at night. Sometimes it ends at two, but more and more often, it starts earlier and ends later. Actually, I'm often not sure of when it ends."

"You black out?"

Claudia nodded. "Yes, I believe I do. At first I thought I was passing out, but then I would find myself waking up in different clothes than I had been wearing the night before. My credit card statement would show purchases—at bars and restaurants—that I had no memory of making. And, worst of all, I was obviously driving my car *somewhere*, as I would wake to find I'd used gas and added miles to the odometer."

"So, when the police asked you about your whereabouts..." Leah began.

"I had to tell them that I don't remember what I don't remember," Claudia said. "Because I honestly don't remember."

She finally looked up from her empty teacup, tears forming in the corners of her eyes.

"Did I kill Ronald Hatchet? I don't know. It seems unlikely, but I'd have to admit that my short relationship with him was similarly unlikely."

She shook her head and Leah realized for the first time just how frightened the older woman was.

"I just don't know," she said again as the tears, which had been impending, finally arrived.

CHAPTER SEVENTEEN

The next morning, Leah took her first ride on St. Paul's Green Line. She was surprised she hadn't taken advantage of the train before, as the light rail system–which stopped right outside her door–conveniently dropped her off a mere two blocks from the theater.

She tried to use this travel time to review her lines—again—for that night's Pay What You Can performance, but instead she spent most of the short trip thinking about Claudia Moffatt. In fact, despite her best efforts to the contrary, the older woman's odd, unresolved confession from the night before continued to haunt her throughout her entire work day.

She might have lost the whole day to this reverie, except she needed to oversee the workman who had been hired to install the surveillance cameras over the theater's front and back doors.

His name was Norm and he was round and jovial and quite talkative. He was intrigued with the theater and after he had installed the two wireless cameras, he spent the next hour or so in Leah's office, getting the service set-up on her computer. And talking to her about theater. In fact, most of the time, it seemed, was spent talking about theater.

"I was in the Senior Class play in high school," he said with a grin as he installed the new software on her desktop computer.

He had commandeered her chair, so Leah was leaning on the credenza behind her desk. She considered going somewhere else—maybe hanging out in Betsy's office for the duration—but she felt she should probably stick around while a strange man had access to the theater's computer system. Although *system* was a strong word.

But her computer did have all the budgets for the theater, along with bank account numbers and other data that–while not strictly sensitive–was really not for public consumption.

And so she stayed and leaned and listened to Norm.

"It was a silly damned play," Norm continued while he clicked away with the mouse and typed an occasional serial number on the keyboard. "It was called *The Skin of Our Teeth*," he continued, and then turned to Leah. "Have you heard of it?"

Leah nodded. "Yes. It's by Thornton Wilder," she said. "He also wrote *Our Town*."

"Well, I don't know about that," Norm said as he turned back to his work. "But *The Skin of Our Teeth* was weird."

Leah had studied the play back in college and although she remembered reading several lengthy critical discussions of the play, she had to agree with Norm's pithy assessment. "Yes," she said. "It is weird."

"So then, for a couple years," Norm continued, "the wife and I got season tickets to some theater over in Minneapolis, what's it called?"

"There are several," Leah began, but Norm cut her off.

"Well, we made it–just barely–through the first two plays and then we gave the rest of the season tickets to my artsy neighbor. We just didn't get what they were doing. Rave reviews but we just didn't get it."

Leah smiled at this assessment and wondered which of the multiple small theater companies in Minneapolis had left Norm and his wife so baffled.

"The thing was," Norm said as he turned away from the keyboard, "we just got the sense that the actors on stage were having more fun than we were having. And while I don't begrudge anyone having a good time, I also don't want to pay for two pricey tickets–and then get hammered fifteen bucks for parking–to watch somebody else have a good time."

"That makes perfect sense," Leah agreed.

"What we do love, though, is that dinner theater. The one in Chanhassen. What's that one called?"

"The Chanhassen Dinner Theater?" Leah offered.

Norm clapped his hands together. "That's the one. Now that's one we like. You have a nice dinner, maybe a steak, maybe some chicken. A glass of wine or a beer. You watch the show– they sing, they dance–then comes intermission. Another beer, maybe a nice piece of cheesecake. Then the second act, the boy gets the girl and everybody goes home happy. That's what I call good theater."

"I really can't argue with that," Leah said and she was telling the truth. For a brief moment, she considered asking Norm to come in and have a long talk with the folks on the Play Selection Committee. But the day was slipping away and she did have work to do.

"Anyway, about the surveillance system…" she began, but Norm held up a hand.

"We're all set to go here," Norm said as he stood up and gestured for Leah to take back her chair. "Let me walk you through it."

Happily, Norm's explanation on how to operate the surveillance system was only about half as long and far less detailed than his discussion about the local theater scene.

"It's basically self-working," he explained as Leah looked at her computer screen. It looked exactly the same as when Norm had started the installation. Nothing appeared to have changed.

"Why don't I see anything," Leah asked, looking down at the keyboard to see if it would provide an explanation.

"The system is motion-sensitive," Norm said. "It doesn't pop on until it detects motion by one of the doors. Because it's motion activated, it doesn't put hours and hours of nothing on your hard drive. Or, actually in this case, up in the cloud."

"You've lost me already."

As if the computer realized Leah was in desperate need of a visual explanation, at that moment a video image appeared on her screen. It was a high-angle view from over the front door of the theater; Betsy had stepped up to the door and was putting her key in the lock.

"Okay," Norm said as he leaned forward. "Now you're seeing the system in action. The camera detected the motion of that woman coming up to the door—"

"That's Betsy, she's the Admin here," Leah explained.

"Okay, so the system saw the motion of Betsy the Admin," Norm continued. "That triggered the system to put the image up on your computer, to notify you that someone is here. And it also triggered the RECORD function," he added, pointing to a small flashing red dot in the corner of the video screen.

On the screen, Betsy had completed her unlocking of the front door and had disappeared from the camera's view.

"The system will record as long as it detects motion and then will revert to the earlier, passive mode until it senses motion again," Norm said.

He gathered some product brochures that had come with the cameras, straightened them into a neat stack and handed the pile to Leah. Then he turned and began to pack up his tools.

"There's a website link in that Welcome Packet where you can go and see some other videos on all the specifics of the system: How to transfer files, how to download files, how to erase files. But I think you understand the basics."

"Yes, I think I do," Leah said as she continued to look at the video image, which now just showed the front steps of the theater from the camera's perch above the front door. A moment later, the image disappeared and the red light went out. "And the back door camera…?"

"Set up the same as this one," Norm said. "As soon as someone comes into the camera range, it starts recording, puts a time stamp on it, saves it to the cloud, just like the one by the front door."

"And you'll put the same program on Betsy's computer, so that she can see when people come and go?"

"Sure thing," Norm said. He had gathered all his tools and stood by the door, awaiting further direction. "And–getting back to our theater discussion–if you guys serve a nice meal and do musicals, I'd be happy to take a brochure home to the little woman."

"Well, Norm, I'm sorry to report that we hardly ever do musicals, and we don't offer food service," Leah said as she instinctively reached for a season brochure. "But I can make this promise to you: It's our goal that the audience <u>always</u> has as much fun as the people on stage. Or more."

"That's all I'm asking for," Norm said with a wide grin as he took the brochure from her. "That's all anyone's asking for. Now point me toward Betsy the Admin."

* * *

Leah was still thinking about her conversation with Norm several hours later. She had just settled into her spot in front of the makeup mirror and had started to unscrew the caps of the line of small jars in front of her. She thought about how important it was for small theaters to hear that sort of feedback from their audiences and began to consider ways of doing that for the Como Lake Players. It may require, she thought with a smile, the creation of yet another committee.

She could hear Monica and Lucas discussing the finer points of sense memory on the other side of the room, but she was the only actor on her side. Doris had not yet arrived, which was a little strange as the older woman was usually there well ahead of her.

Leah glanced over at Doris's workspace, which was neat and orderly, with (as her father used to say) a place for everything and everything in its place. She saw that Doris had posted some snapshots on her mirror and realized she hadn't noticed that before. She looked at her own mirror, to see if Joan O'Malley had done the same, but the area was free of any personalization by the now-hospitalized actress.

Leah glanced over to the other side of the room and even though Monica was partially blocking the view, she could see that the younger actress had adorned her mirror with a wide range of photos and clippings. Leah turned to look over at Lucas's mirror and recognized immediately the single image the Method actor had placed on his mirror. It was Marlon Brando.

"So if I'm playing Joan of Arc, how am I supposed to create the sense memory of being burned at the stake?" Monica said, a hint of frustration in her voice. "That's completely outside the realm of my experience."

"It's a simple matter of extrapolation," Lucas said.

His tone—which had a particularly strong, familiar stench of patronization to it—provided Leah with a sense memory of her own: She immediately flashed back on the countless similar conversations she'd had with Dylan.

"Extrapolation?" Monica repeated.

"Look, at some point in your life you must have burned your finger, lighting a candle or taking something out of the oven, right?"

"Yes," Monica said tentatively, clearly thinking this might be some sort of trick question.

"Well, all you do is extrapolate from that," Lucas said. "This is what it felt like when I burned my finger; multiply that by 100, and that's what it would feel like to be engulfed in flames. It's really pretty basic, you know."

Leah was starting to feel engulfed in flames herself, but before she could add her two cents to the younger actors' conversation, her attention was diverted elsewhere.

"Traffic was just nutty tonight, did you find that to be the case? Or maybe it's just because I'm not used to getting here at this time on a Monday night." The voice came from behind her and Leah turned to see that Doris was taking off her coat as she headed toward her spot in front of the mirror.

"I've been here all day," Leah said as she adjusted her chair to make room for the older actress.

"Oh, of course you have, poor thing," Doris said as she set her large purse on the floor under the makeup table. "I forgot that you're doing double duty. You must be exhausted."

"It's been a long day," Leah agreed. "But things get back to normal tomorrow."

"Until the weekend," Doris said with a short laugh as she settled into her chair.

"Yes, next weekend," Leah repeated. She still hadn't determined what the plan would be for those three shows.

"You interruptible?"

Leah turned to see that Kanisha was standing there, clipboard in hand. "Sure, what's up?"

"Two things. First, someone has been into the prop food again."

"Again? Do we need to put it under lock and key?"

"That might be advisable," the Stage Manager said with a shake of her head. "I can scrounge together what we need for tonight, but the spread that Aunt Abby and Aunt Martha put out will continue to look a little on the skimpy side."

"Okay, thanks. I'll send out another threatening email to the cast and crew. What was the second thing?"

Kanisha had started to walk away. She stopped, thinking for a long moment. "Oh, that detective guy is here," she finally said. "He wanted to know if you have a minute?"

Leah looked into the mirror, quickly assessing the lack of progress she had made. She had not yet begun the aging process on her face. "I don't know, do I?"

Kanisha glanced at her watch. "Plenty of time. The outer lobby is filling up, but we haven't opened the back lobby or the house yet."

"Great," Leah said as she stood up.

Kanisha turned and headed back the way she had come. Leah was about to follow her, then stopped and returned to her mirror. She gave herself a quick once-over.

"You look terrific," Doris said with a smile. "Not to worry."

Leah continued to look in the mirror. "I don't know about that," she said, "but for now this is the best I can do."

She moved quickly toward the steep stairs that would take her up to the lobby.

CHAPTER EIGHTEEN

"Can you point out which ones are the undercover detectives?"

Detective Albertson chuckled at Leah's question. "It sort of defeats the purpose of them being undercover," he said with a smile, "if I point them out to you."

"Sure, that makes sense," Leah agreed. They were both peering through a curtain which separated the box office lobby–where all the ticket buyers were currently standing–from the main lobby which would funnel them into the theater.

"The reason I'm bothering you is, the sign says 'Pay What You Can,'" Detective Albertson continued. "And my guys are wondering how much that should be?"

"Oh, your men don't need to pay," Leah said as she closed the gap in the curtain to stay out of the line of sight from the outer lobby. She wasn't in costume or makeup, yet, but still didn't want to be seen by the audience in her current state. "I'll have Betsy comp them in. They just need to identify themselves at the box office."

Albertson shook his head. "Sorry, but like I said, tonight is strictly an undercover operation, designed to protect you," he said. "We're not announcing our presence to anyone, including the box office staff."

Leah considered this. "All right," she said. "In that case, they can–as the sign suggests–pay whatever they can. Or want to."

Albertson pulled out his trusty notepad. "And how much is that? On average?"

Leah smiled. "Well, this is my first time with this theater, but they tell me there can be quite a range," she said. "The poor actor types tend to pay five dollars, maybe ten."

Albertson made a note of this. "Ten dollars," he repeated. "Is that about average?"

Leah shook her head. "No, because long-time patrons sometimes use the occasion to make a substantial donation to the theater. For example, if they liked a production, they might come back on a Pay What You Can night and write a check for a thousand dollars."

"Really?"

Leah nodded. "They tell me that a couple years back, a family used the Pay What You Can night to deliver their mother's bequest of a check for fifty thousand dollars."

Albertson responded to this news with a low whistle. "I can see why you didn't want to cancel this show," he said.

"Yes, trite as it sounds, in order for the theater to go on," Leah said. "the show must go on as well."

He snapped his notebook shut. "All right, then," he said as he neatly slid it into his coat's inside pocket. "You just act like everything is normal."

"I'm not that good an actress," Leah said as she turned to head toward the door to the basement.

"Is that self-deprecation I hear?" came a voice from behind her. She turned to see that Alex had come in through the back door and was also headed toward the doorway to the theater's basement. "No talk like that on a show day," he said, his voice bellowing like Walter Matthau in *The Sunshine Boys*. "Never on a show day!"

Leah turned to Detective Albertson. "Alex is determined to keep me positive throughout this trying time," she explained. "He was the one who helped get me up to speed on the part on such short notice. He also plays Dr. Einstein in the play," she added.

"Ah, I thought you looked familiar," Albertson said. "I've seen the show. Very funny stuff."

Alex nodded at the compliment. "Thanks," he said. "But I've got to get downstairs and sign in, or one Stage Manager in particular is going to have my butt in a sling."

Leah glanced at her watch. "Oh, goodness, I have to finish getting ready," she said as she turned to follow Alex. She looked back at Detective Albertson. "Well, thanks for–I don't know what to thank you for, but thank you!"

"No problem," Albertson said. He turned to head back toward the box office, while Alex and Leah dove toward the stairs.

"Is he a cop?" Alex said as they scurried down the steep steps toward the dressing rooms.

"I can neither confirm nor deny," she said as she passed him and made a beeline toward her makeup table. Alex stopped at the bulletin board to put a checkmark by his name on the cast sign-in sheet and then hustled over to his own makeup table to begin his transformation into Dr. Einstein.

* * *

"Third time's the charm," Alex said with a grin as Leah passed him on her way up to the stage. She was now fully made-up and costumed. Just as she had done for her first two performances, she clutched her script tightly in her hand. Although she also noticed that tonight she held it with something less than her traditional death grip.

"Break a leg," Leah replied with a smile and then realized she was about to step over the spot where Joan O'Malley had done exactly that three nights earlier. Double that, actually, with two broken legs and a concussion. Leah shuddered as she stepped over the spot at the base of the stairs, realizing again just how much worse it could have been for her predecessor in the role of

Aunt Abby. She made her way up to the backstage area and gave her script one last cursory look as she prepared to step out on stage.

* * *

Moments later, the play began for what was now Leah's third performance in the part.

"Perhaps Alex was right," Leah thought to herself about five minutes into the first act. "Maybe the third time is the charm."

She immediately regretted the thought, knowing that expressing such a positive idea was the fastest way to jinx the entire enterprise. But she couldn't help but let her mind wander–if only a little–because Aunt Abby's lines were coming to her more easily than at the previous two performances, requiring little or no mental effort on her part.

At one point she snuck a look out into the house, thinking she might be able to spot the plain-clothes cops that Detective Albertson had brought with him. But with the exception of the first two rows, the house was a dark gray, blurry mass. She returned her attention back to the stage just in time to deliver her next line to Elaine *("Why don't you sit down, dear?"),* and then began to think about why those plain-clothes detectives were at the show in the first place.

Was there truly someone attending this performance who wanted her out of this play so badly that her life was actually in danger?

The bizarre death of the critic, Ronald Hatchet, had proven that someone harbored–at the very least–a strong grudge against the highly-opinionated reviewer. But was it about this play, or was it personal and unrelated? She considered her encounter with the frazzled Claudia Moffatt, who had no memory of her actions during the time of Hatchet's death. Was she responsible?

And was Hatchet's murderer the same person who had pushed Joan O'Malley down the back stairs, if in fact it was anything more than an accident on the part of the older actress?

And was that the same person who had sent Leah the threatening text? Were all three incidents truly connected, or was this a false assumption she (and Detective Albertson) shouldn't be making? And if it was, what other false assumptions was she operating under?

For the first time, Leah considered the implications of this. If Hatchet's murder wasn't connected to Joan O'Malley's accident, then it was reasonable to consider that it wasn't connected to the threatening text. What if there was no connection between the three incidents? What if Joan's accident was just that–an accident–and what if the text was just a prank?

What if all three events weren't connected but only *seemed* connected? How did that change her perspective on the incidents and what did it do to the very limited list of suspects she currently was considering?

She wanted to delve into this thought further, but unfortunately Aunt Abby had a bunch of lines to deliver and that wouldn't happen if Leah didn't utter them. So Leah returned her full attention to the play as it moved slowly, steadily toward intermission.

* * *

"All clear here."

That was the text Leah found waiting for her from Detective Albertson when she picked up her phone at the end of Act One. She wasn't entirely sure she understood what those enigmatic three words meant, but at least it sounded positive.

"Ditto backstage," she texted quickly, and then headed downstairs to refresh her makeup and make a quick trip to the bathroom before the start of Act Two.

"It's a lively audience tonight," Doris said as Leah slid into the chair in front of her mirror. Leah glanced over at Doris, who was just finishing her own touch-up. "It's fun when the house is filled with a lot of actors."

"Actors and benefactors," Leah said. "I can't wait to check in with Betsy and see what the final tally is for the night."

"Sorry I was late with that one cue," Monica said as she approached the makeup table. "I don't know where my head was at. My brother and sister-in-law are here tonight and I think it's freaking me out a bit."

"Not a problem," Leah said reassuringly. She gestured over toward Doris. "Aunt Martha was able to fix it on the fly and the audience was none the wiser.'

"Having family members in the audience always throws me, too," Doris said. "That's why I always tell family, 'Take my comps, come whenever you want, I just don't want to know about it.'"

"Ignorance is definitely bliss in that regard," Leah agreed. She thought back to when she'd spotted Dylan in the audience during the show on Saturday night and how much it had rattled her. She looked back up at Monica.

"Anyway, don't worry about the cue. You'll get it next time," Leah said as she flashed her a warm smile.

The young actress nodded in agreement and turned to go, then turned back. She hesitated a moment before speaking again. "Will that next time include you?" she asked. Her tone made it clear that an affirmative answer was what she hoped to hear.

The question must have been one that was of interest to the entire cast, as Leah noticed that both Clyde Henderson and Stuart Wilde turned from their positions playing cards on the couch. The cops–Brophy, Klein and O'Hara–also stopped what they were doing to hear her response. Even Lucas paused in his makeup touch-up and looked at her via his mirror from across the room.

"Well," Leah began, not really certain what her answer should be. She was sure that Detective Albertson would advise against it, but he was still working from the premise that the threatening text had been serious and not just a prank. For her part, Leah no longer thought it was an actual threat.

Plus, as difficult as it was for her to admit it, deep down she was really enjoying playing the role and performing in the play. Now that the initial panic about remembering lines and learning blocking had passed, she found she was loving her time on stage and wasn't really in a terrific hurry to see it end.

"I'm really not entirely sure yet," she finally said, saying it as much to the whole room as to Monica. And to herself.

This wishy-washy answer was met with a collective moan from the rest of the actors. Their lamentations were cut short by Kanisha as she entered with her call of "Five minutes!"

The drama with Leah momentarily forgotten, the cast echoed her words back to the Stage Manager and then scrambled to finish their various intermission tasks before heading back up to the stage.

* * *

Act Two was just as strong–in many ways, stronger–than the first act. At least, that's the way it felt to Leah. The audience of theater folks and benefactors loved the in-jokes about Mortimer being a drama critic, and the menacing scenes between brothers Jonathan and Mortimer really crackled with tension.

And, of course, Alex killed as Dr. Einstein. He had even found a way to get a laugh with something as simple as trying to put his watch back into his vest pocket. From her side of the stage, Leah had trouble not cracking a smile at his actions, which had evolved from night to night into a small comic gem.

The show ended with a rousing standing ovation and the bubbly cast made record time getting out of their costumes and back up to the lobby to greet their enthusiastic friends.

Leah and Doris didn't make the same mad dash to the lobby, but instead moved at their normal pace as they removed their makeup and hung their costumes up on the rack for the necessary cleaning before next weekend's shows.

"Are you headed over to Jimmy's?" Doris asked as she put on her coat and grabbed her purse from under her makeup table.

"I'm not sure," Leah admitted. "I need to talk to Betsy, to find out what tonight's take was."

"Well, if I don't see you there, I hope to see you back here on Thursday for the speed-through," she said with a smile as she headed toward the stairs. "And maybe this week, the speed-through won't take longer than the show!"

With that she turned and headed up the stairs. Leah smiled, noting that Doris's remark was perhaps the strongest comment the older actress had yet made about working with the difficult Joan O'Malley.

Minutes later Leah found herself pushing her way through the crowded lobby, finally making her way to the door to the box office. Before she could reach for the doorknob, she felt a light tap on her shoulder. She turned to see Detective Albertson looking down at her.

"Hey, how did your guys like the show?" she asked, still feeling giddy from the standing ovation and the energy emanating from the lobby.

"Well, they weren't here to critique it," he said as he suppressed a smile. "But I will say that nothing unplanned happened on stage. Or in the auditorium. And they were very happy about that. How much longer do you expect this crowd to linger?"

He turned and looked over his shoulder. The cast and their acting friends still filled the small lobby to capacity, although Leah noted that some small groups were inching toward the door.

"I suspect this group will move, *en masse*, over to Jimmy's within a few minutes. I'm planning to join them, if you're interested." Leah tried to make this last suggestion sound as off-handed as possible, but felt that she hadn't really pulled it off.

For his part, Detective Albertson looked dismayed. Leah couldn't tell if it was due to her suggestion, the size of the crowd in the lobby, or some combination of the two.

"Moving from one crowded room to another?" he said flatly.

"That's not ideal. Is there any way you could give it a miss tonight?"

"Look, Detective Albertson–Mark–I have to tell you, I'm really not convinced that there is anything behind that text I got," she said. "While I appreciate your efforts on my behalf, I think it was just a prank."

"You may be right," he said with a nod. "However, given the recent events, I believe we need to treat any threat as real until it's proven otherwise. And that particular text has yet to be proven otherwise."

Before she could respond, there was a sudden flurry of activity as Gloria picked that moment to burst out of the box office.

"There you are! Honey, the theater had quite a night. What a show!"

"I didn't realize you were here tonight," Leah said.

"I second-acted the show," Gloria said. "We had a big wine and cheese and wine thing over at my place of employment, but I just had to see how we did tonight, box office-wise."

"And how did we do?" Leah asked. While she was both excited and nervous to hear the final tally, she could tell that her friend had clearly indulged in a lot of the wine and perhaps not quite enough of the cheese.

"Well, as you know, we had hoped to make enough tonight to cover the cost of a new boiler for the furnace," Gloria began. "And although this is unofficial, I think I can safely report that we have achieved the boiler. Plus new flashing for the roof."

Leah held up her arms, preparing to cheer, but Gloria held up her hand to stop her.

"And," Gloria added, pausing dramatically, "there is a very good chance we can replace the floor tile in <u>both</u> the Men's and Ladies' rooms."

"Wow," Leah said. "It's like Christmas came early this year."

"Yes," Gloria agreed. "And Santa brought his tool belt. Let's go celebrate." She grabbed Leah's arm, but was met with immediate resistance.

"Detective Albertson would prefer that I forgo the evening's festivities," Leah said as she gently removed her friend's hand from her arm. "In light of recent events and text threats and all."

"Oh, poppycock," Gloria said, waving away the idea with her now free hand. "And this is coming from someone who never uses the word poppycock when something far more offensive will suffice." She looked up at Detective Albertson, who appeared to be amused at her slightly-tipsy behavior. "Look, Inspector Dilbertson," she began.

'Detective Albertson," Leah quickly corrected.

'Whatever," Gloria said. "Al. I can take perfectly good care of our mutual–and adorable and single– friend Leah, so you don't have to worry, as she's in good hands. Those hands being mine," she added.

Detective Albertson began to reply, but Gloria cut him off. "Or, better yet, why don't you join us? You know what they say, 'Two's company, three's really interesting.'"

This last remark produced a burst of laughter from Gloria, along with slightly embarrassed smiles from both Leah and Detective Albertson.

"Look," Albertson finally said. "I don't want to interfere with your day-to-day life. If you want to go to this bar and then home, I'll just ask one of my men to keep an eye on you. They don't have to be intrusive, they just have to be able to see you until you're safely at home. They won't get in your way at all."

"Thanks for being so flexible," Leah said.

"Very flexible," Gloria added with a leer.

Before she could utter anything else, suggestive or otherwise, Leah pulled a giggling Gloria toward the front door and the two women stumbled into the cool night air.

CHAPTER NINETEEN

"This is ridiculous," Alex said.

Leah nodded in agreement. "Although I don't think it's mean-spirited. I think it's more out of habit than anything else."

"What are you two goons talking about? And where's our waitress?" Gloria's limited interest in their conversation immediately dissipated when she spotted a server two tables over. She gave her a friendly if desperate wave.

"The self-segregation of these actors," Leah said. "They gather at different tables, based solely on age."

She glanced over and realized instantly that Gloria wasn't listening, but was instead trying to get the waitress's attention. If she'd had a flare gun, Leah had little doubt that Gloria would have used it at this moment to place her drink order.

"This situation requires a bold act," Alex said. He turned to Leah. "Are you with me?"

"Sure, up to a point." Leah said. "What's the plan?"

"Follow me."

With that, Alex got up and strode decisively toward the table with the young actors. Leah followed, turning back to make sure Gloria wasn't wobbling after them.

Alex stood by the table, pushing himself between two of the

chairs. "Can you guys give me a hand?" His request was completely off-the-cuff and casual.

"Sure, what's up?" Brophy asked.

"This table. Stand up and give me a hand." With that, Alex grabbed the edge of the table and began to lift it off the ground. This caused several glasses on the table to begin to slide precariously toward the edge. To prevent that, Brophy and Klein both stood up and grabbed their side of the table, leveling it as they lifted it up.

"Walk this way," Alex said, and with that he started walking backwards across the room. The two actors followed, forcing the others to stand and trail behind them.

Leah saw where this was headed and made a beeline toward the table with the older actors. Without saying anything to the small group, she gestured to Stuart Wilde–who was seated at the head of the table–to get up. Thinking he was doing this to give Leah his seat, he graciously stood up and waved her toward his chair.

Leah slid the chair out of the way just as Alex and his reluctant co-movers arrived. Alex positioned the new table alongside the old one and moments later all the actors from *Arsenic and Old Lace*–young and old–were seated at the same long set of tables.

"There," Alex said conclusively as he pulled up a chair, placing himself on the demarcation point between the two tables. "Was that so difficult?"

"They're still segregated by tables," Leah pointed out as she pulled up a chair and sat across from him. "But now at least the tables are connected.

"Baby steps," Alex suggested. "Baby steps."

Leah spent a full five minutes in conversation at the new table arrangement before she remembered with a sudden start that she had virtually abandoned Gloria at their original location. She jumped up and scrambled toward her friend across the room, only to discover that the highly voluble Gloria was deep in conversation with a group of college guys at the next table.

It took considerable persuasion on Leah's part to separate

Gloria from the boisterous bunch and steer her to the new table amalgamation Alex had created. Much of the short trip consisted of Gloria's mixed pride and antipathy at being referred to as a 'cougar' by the guys at the table.

"I'm not old enough to be a cougar, am I?" she pleaded several times as Leah helped navigate her across the room. "Is a cougar older than a Mrs. Robinson?"

"I think Mrs. Robinson is considered the original cougar," Leah suggested as she steered her tipsy friend to the table. Once there, she held on to her with one hand while pulling a spare chair over with the other. She got Gloria safely into the chair and put what was left of her most current drink in front of her, and then returned to her own seat.

"Sure, you can block your phone number when you're sending a text," a voice was saying as Leah settled in. "It's a piece of cake."

She looked over to see that Monica was talking to O'Hara, the youngest of the police officers in the show and the only female among the three cops.

"That would be great," the young woman said. She shifted her voice down to just above a whisper. "I want to catfish my brother, to get back at him for a prank he played on me."

"It's super simple," Monica said. She gestured toward Lucas, who was deep in conversation with Eddie, the actor who played Teddy. "Lucas did it for me, to help me get rid of this creep who was cyber-stalking me."

"What did I do?" Lucas said. His eyebrows had shot up at the mention of his name.

"She needs to know how to send a text without giving away your phone number," Monica said as she jerked her head toward O'Hara. "I told her you could show her how."

Lucas put up his hands and then lowered them toward the table. He lowered his voice to a similar degree. "Hey, don't be spreading that around," he said quietly. "That's not for public consumption."

He glanced around the table and for a brief second his eyes

connected with Leah's. She did her best to give the impression that she hadn't been listening but was just idly looking around the table. Lucas looked away from her and leaned in toward Monica. A moment later, O'Hara joined them in their hushed conversation.

Leah glanced toward them one last time, but their voices were lost in the overall hubbub of the bar. So she turned her attention back to Gloria, who was in the midst of asking some of the older actors what age range they felt best designated a cougar.

* * *

It took a little longer than Leah had anticipated, but in less than 30 minutes it felt like they were all sitting at the same table. The actors–young and old alike–were trading war stories of bungled auditions and missed cues and after a couple departures and one or two new arrivals, suddenly the long table seemed entirely integrated.

"Nice job," Leah said to Alex as he slid back into his seat across from her. He had a new drink in one hand and a fresh bowl of pretzels in the other.

"Thanks, but I've been carrying pretzels since I was twenty," he said as he set the bowl on the table. Hands reached out from all sides for the salty treats. "I once considered it as a possible career."

"Until the alluring siren call of accounting beckoned?" Leah suggested.

"Yes, the numbers game, she is a fickle mistress," he replied dramatically. "Not for the faint of heart or those suffering the painful anguish of Dyscalculia." He recognized the look of confusion on Leah's face, and so he quickly added, "That is, Dyslexia with numbers."

"Ah," she said. "Anyway, what I meant was, nice job on getting these two groups together."

She glanced around the table, which was now comprised of

numerous multi-generational conversations. Doris was talking with Monica and O'Hara about the difficulties of playing Juliet ("That girl is really just a soppy mess," the older actress confided as the two young women nodded in agreement), while Clyde Henderson was explaining to Brophy and Rooney the secret of getting cast after a call-back ("I always wear exactly the same thing I wore to the audition," he said with a wink. "My logic is that if they liked me before, it could just as easily been because of my wardrobe as anything else.")

Leah looked back at Alex, but he was now engaged in a quiet and serious-looking conversation with Lucas. She couldn't hear what they were saying, but they both wore intense expressions. Lucas glanced over at her for a split second, then looked guiltily away.

Suddenly Leah remembered the plainclothes detectives that Detective Albertson had assigned to her. She scanned the bar, wondering if one or more had followed her over from the theater. She didn't see any familiar faces, but realized immediately that was the point. She wasn't *supposed* to see them, if in fact they were out there. Still, it was fun to look at the faces to see who might seem out of place in this lively bar.

The bar had become so lively, in fact, that it took a moment to recognize that her name was being called out.

"Leah, they're calling your name," Gloria said, giving her friend's arm an unnecessary punch. "Apparently, it's time for a toast." Gloria already had her half-empty glass posed elegantly in her other hand. She nodded toward the head of the table.

Clyde Henderson, the actor who played Mr. Witherspoon, was standing, also holding a glass in his hand, although his was significantly more full than Gloria's.

"I was just saying," Clyde said, once he felt he had the entire table's attention, "that I think a toast is in order. I was asked to wait until Stuart had completed an accompanying limerick, but word from him is that the verse, in fact, is slow in coming."

Stuart looked up from the pile of crushed and scribbled

napkins in front of him. "Still can't find a decent rhyme for 'arsenic,'" he growled, which produced a knowing laugh from the ensemble. Apparently this had been an issue for Stuart throughout the run of the show. "Why couldn't we have done *Barefoot in the Park*?" he said as he continued to scribble away.

Clyde treated the question as strictly rhetorical and continued on with his impromptu speech.

"Anyhoo," he said, "I'd like us all to raise a glass to our intrepid Aunt Abby, who weathered the most-frightening of all actor's nightmares with grace and aplomb. Here's to our one-and-only, Leah Sexton!"

Clyde raised his glass and the table erupted in an enthusiastic if poorly-synchronized rendition of "Hear-hear!" This was followed by a few calls of 'Speech, speech!"

Leah nodded at the group. "Thank you, Clyde," she said as she looked to the head of the table. "And thanks to Stuart for the attempt."

"It's not dead yet," he said breathlessly without looking up. "Not dead yet."

"And thanks to all of you, for your help and support during this past weekend. I couldn't have done it without you. Literally."

This produced a laugh from the group and then there was a long moment of silence while everyone took a sip from their drink. The quiet was broken by a loud question from the only one who wasn't strictly part of the group.

"Are you gonna do it again?" Gloria nearly shouted after she had polished off her drink and slammed it dramatically on the table. "Will you be gracing our stage next weekend or not?"

As Leah fumbled to assemble a response to this question for the second time in one night, she scanned all the faces at the table. They looked–individually and collectively–hopeful.

"Oh, I do hope you can," Doris said breathlessly. "It's been so much fun."

"A delight," Clyde added. "A delight."

"And if you don't, what happens to the show?" Monica asked. "Do we get a new Aunt Abby by next Friday or does the show …?" Her voice trailed off and it was clear she didn't want to utter the word 'close' aloud.

The implications of her aborted sentence produced a series of "Oohs" and "Nooos" from around the table. Leah held up her hand.

"Nothing that drastic will happen, I'm sure," she said, her tone lacking the conviction she had hoped for. Her shortage of confidence was apparent in the expressions she got back as she scanned the table. She then continued to look around the room, once again trying to see if she could spot one of the elusive plain-clothes detectives.

"Of course I'm doing it again," she finally said as she turned back to the table. "This weekend, next weekend, closing weekend. I'm in it for the long haul."

This produced cheers all around and Leah turned to see Alex and Doris both smiling back at her broadly. Before she could add anything to her announcement, a shout came from the other end of the table.

"You know what?" Stuart said as he looked up from the pile of crumpled napkins in front of him. "I think I'm going to have more luck if I try to rhyme using the word 'lace!'"

With that, he grabbed a fresh napkin and began to scribble anew.

Leah had heard the expression 'they poured her into a taxi cab' for years; however, she had never experienced that situation in real life. But, like her friend had done for her so many times in the past, Gloria brought that expression to life and then some.

As far as Leah was concerned, the night was over, but apparently Gloria held an entirely contrary opinion. She wanted to hear the words "Last call!" before she'd consider heading out, and even those words could well be open to interpretation and subsequent argument.

With the help of Alex, Leah was able to get the unsteady and belligerent Gloria to the bar's front door with more effort than she had anticipated. Thankfully, what Gloria possessed in determination she lacked in motor skills, and so Alex and Leah were able to get Gloria into a waiting taxi. Leah gave the driver the address, pre-paid for the ride and then included an extra twenty to ensure the wobbly woman made it safely into her condo.

Once the cab was out of sight, Leah and Alex headed across the street to the theater's parking lot. Other cast members were also wandering toward their cars, so the small crowd made the murky lot seem less eerie and threatening than it sometimes felt. Leah made a mental note to add increased parking lot lighting to the budget wish list she was preparing for next year.

As they strolled slowly through the lot, Leah and Alex chatted about the events of the evening and their success at bringing the two sets of actors together. Before she knew it, they had made it to the driver's door of her sad little car. She pulled her keys from her purse on the first try and then turned to Alex.

"All right, I guess that's it until the speed-through on Thursday," she said, for the first time feeling a tinge of awkwardness around Alex. She didn't know if it was the dark parking lot, the events of the past few days or just some unknown hunch. But as the other actors disappeared into their cars, she suddenly wanted to be in hers as well.

"Sure thing," he said. "Let me know if you want to run lines or anything before that."

"I will," she said. "I will."

She knew she should have used that moment to turn and unlock her car door, but she hesitated and suddenly Alex was kissing her. It wasn't a mashing kiss and, in its way, it was far from unpleasant. But it was sudden and surprising and not what she needed right now. She pushed him away with an abruptness that surprised her.

"No, Alex," she stuttered. "I'm sorry, it's just. Not now."

Alex stumbled back, holding up his hands for balance as well as in protest. "No, my bad," he said quickly. "My bad. I misread the thing and I shouldn't have," he continued, searching for the words to make this right. He couldn't find them.

"I just can't right now," Leah repeated as she jerked the car door open. She slid into the front seat and started the engine with far less clumsiness than she had anticipated. She flipped on the headlights, revealing that at least three of the other actors–Monica, Lucas and Teddy–had witnessed at least part of her awkward exchange with Alex.

Leah slammed the door and hit the gas, passing Alex and the other actors in the dim parking lot as she made her way toward the exit.

Just as she turned left, she noticed a figure standing in the shadows by the theater. Yet another person who had witnessed her debacle, she thought. But when she looked again, he was gone.

"If that's one of my plainclothes protectors, where was he thirty seconds ago?" Leah mumbled, and then turned her attention toward the road and navigating the short trip back home. She was still coming down from the momentary panic of the attempted kiss, realizing that she had only met Alex mere days ago. And, of course, there was the murder of the critic, the actress's accident and the threatening text.

All in all, she decided, this was not the right time to start a new relationship. And if it was the right time, Alex was absolutely not the right guy. Or at least, that's the way it felt tonight.

The short drive was consumed with these thoughts, and before she knew it, she was headed into her condo's underground garage. She was relieved–and not for the first time–that her underground parking spot got her into the protection of the building without even needing to step out of her car. The garage, which was better-lit than most, still offered its own sense of creeping dread, so she parked close to the elevator and wasted little time exiting the car and getting into the building.

However, she didn't begin to feel even a little relaxed until she was in her apartment, with the front door firmly locked and bolted. And even then, her sense of apprehension never really left her as she finally drifted off into an uneasy sleep.

CHAPTER TWENTY

Thankfully, Tuesday was an extremely busy day, which gave Leah little time to consider the events of the previous night. Or the events of the preceding weekend for that matter.

First there was the issue of the annual budget, which she was due to present to the Board at the upcoming Board meeting, an event which appeared to be approaching at light speed.

She spent the morning juggling numbers, trying to find a reasonable way to add one part-time employee and still make all the figures add up to the surprisingly small number she had been given for running the entire theater.

Since starting this new job, Leah had been pushing hard to hire someone to manage all the volunteers who worked at the theater, as opposed to making that position voluntary as well. Her rationale was that–since it took a surprisingly large number of unpaid people to keep the theater humming along–a paid employee would be far more motivated to find and recruit this plethora of volunteers.

The sheer number of volunteers required on a typical show night–from box office staff to the handful of ushers to the house manager to tech people to the helpers who ran the concession stand—was staggering, particularly when you multiplied it by three shows a week.

Then you had to factor in all the volunteers who worked on the sets, props and costumes for each show. Finding people to fill those positions was becoming harder and harder. And it wasn't made any easier when the person in charge of tracking down all those volunteers was a volunteer as well. Or, as it turned out, a series of volunteers.

According to the theater's records, they'd had five different Volunteer Coordinators in the past eighteen months alone, all of them volunteers. If she could make the numbers work, Leah was sure that a part-time <u>paid</u> employee would be far more effective at bringing in all the unpaid bodies they needed.

When she couldn't get the numbers to quite work for the third time, she set the budget aside to look over the Play Selection Committee's first pass at the recommended plays for the upcoming season. In addition to their list of nine plays, they also included their motives for rejecting some of the suggestions they had been urged to consider.

Leah noted right away the committee had neglected to add any plays by George Bernard Shaw to the season, despite her strong recommendation that it would appease the major donors, Bea and Abe Kaufman. She made a note to suggest they re-look at that decision.

She also noted they had rejected the comedy, *Play It Again, Sam*, because—as one committee member noted in an indignant footnote—the character of Humphrey Bogart suggests in the play that the main character should slap his ex-wife. That same committee, however, seemed to have no problem with a character murdering his wife and had enthusiastically recommended they stage *Dial M For Murder* as the first show in the upcoming season.

While Leah was struggling with that bizarre contradiction, Betsy stopped into her office to wish her good night.

"Is it five o'clock already?" Leah asked as she glanced at the small clock in the corner of her computer screen. The day had flown by so quickly that she hadn't even remembered to stop for lunch.

"It's past five, dear," Betsy said as she pulled on her coat and began the slow process of buttoning it. "You've been so quiet all day, I almost forgot you were in here."

"A deep dive into the budget can do that," Leah said, gesturing at her paper-strewn desk. "And then there's the matter of the Play Selection Committee and their oddball selections."

"Oh, I'm sure that was quite the list," Betsy said with a slow shake of her head. "Don't fret, though. Wiser heads eventually prevail. You just have to wear them down."

"Thanks for the advice," Leah said. "How many rounds do they traditionally do?"

"One year, twenty-two versions of the season were presented before the Board signed off," Betsy said. "Gloria finally just locked the whole darned committee in a room until they came back with an acceptable list.

"And," Betsy added, her voice dropping to a whisper, "I'm not kidding. She actually locked them in a room. It was the furniture storage room. Gloria said they could find several beds in there, along with linens. I think some of the poor dears thought she would leave them in there for days."

"I wouldn't put it past her," Leah said, wondering not for the first time how her friend was feeling after her bout of over-indulgence the night before. She decided a quick phone call might be in order.

"Anyway, I'll lock up on my way out," Betsy said. "Unless you're leaving now?" she added hopefully.

"No, I'm on a roll here," Leah said. "I'm going to give it a couple more hours."

"All right, then," Betsy said as she moved toward the door. "There are no rehearsals scheduled tonight, so you'll be all on your own."

Leah squinted over at the older woman. "I thought we had auditions tonight," she said. "For *Inherit the Wind*."

Betsy shook her head. "Our brilliant young director wasn't

quite ready with the audition sides," she said. "So she asked to move it to next week."

Leah glanced up at the large calendar which hung on the wall across from her desk. It was a detailed overview of the theater's entire season. "She's cutting it sort of close, don't you think? Given the size of that cast?"

"I mentioned that very idea to her," Betsy agreed. "But these young ones often feel they work better under pressure."

"If that were true, I'd be running the Guthrie right now," Leah said with a laugh as she reached for the phone to give Gloria a quick call. "Have a good night."

"See you in the morning, dear," Betsy replied, and moments later she had disappeared out the door.

* * *

"At first I thought the ringing was in my head. Then I realized it was my phone. Although if I listen carefully, I can still hear a ringing in my head."

Leah laughed. "I was wondering why it took so long for you to answer. I thought you'd be at work."

"No," Gloria said, her voice sounding hoarse and thick. "I took a sick day. Actually, I took a *'god, why did I drink so much last night?'* day. So give me an update: Did I do anything worthy of a juicy police report? Or at the very least, an internet meme?"

"No," Leah said with a laugh. "Although I think you might have frightened a bunch of college boys into celibacy. At least temporarily."

"Well, good. So the evening wasn't a complete bust."

"No, not a complete bust," Leah agreed. "But it was weird." As she said this, her attention was drawn to her computer, where a video window had just popped up in the corner of the screen. It was a view from over the theater's front door, showing Betsy as she exited the building. Betsy gave the door a quick tug, to make sure it had locked, before she walked out of frame.

"How so?" Gloria asked.

"Oh, that's a story for another time," Leah said. "Maybe over a couple glasses of wine."

"It's hard for me to say this, but for once that doesn't sound in the least bit appealing."

"So let me ask you a work question," Leah said as she picked up the list of recommendations from the Play Selection Committee. "How do you folks pick your season over at that grown-up theater across the river? Is there a committee?"

"Sure, but it's usually a committee of one," Gloria said. "Usually the Artistic Director generates her list and then the department heads bless it. The only hurdle is occasionally Marketing, but that's only if they think they'll have trouble selling a show. Are you struggling with the Play Selection Committee and their alleged selection process?"

"Yep," Leah said. "I spent the better part of the day working on the budget, so my eyes were already bugging out of my head. And then I saw their list for the first time."

"Let me guess: Lots of big shows, each one with multiple sets, am I right?"

"Absolutely," she said as she glanced down at the stack of budget sheets on the other side of her desk. A thought occurred to her. "You know, years ago Dylan and I had a plan of doing an all-*Hamlet* season. We should try that here."

"How would that work? Nine versions of the same show?"

"No, the idea was to do four *Hamlet*-themed shows, three of which would use the same set," Leah explained. "We'd start with *Hamlet*, of course. And then move onto *Rosencrantz and Guildenstern Are Dead*."

"I see," Gloria said. Her voice had loosened up and she was starting to sound more like herself. "Same set, same characters, same costumes."

"Exactly," Leah said. "Then do Lee Blessing's *Fortinbras*, which picks up at the end of *Hamlet*."

"Again, same set, same cast, same costumes."

"Right. And then round the whole thing out with Paul Rudnick's *I Hate Hamlet*."

"Small cast, contemporary costumes, one set," Gloria added. "That would certainly save a boatload of money, if you could pull it off."

"Well, it's just a thought," Leah said. "Do you guys ever resort to oddball penny-pinching techniques?"

Gloria snorted. "Honey, have you forgotten who you're talking to? Just last month, we had a director who said he wanted to put an actual swimming pool in the center of our proscenium stage."

"That's nuts," Leah said. "How did they break it to him that it wasn't going to happen?"

"That's just it," Gloria said. "Two days later they brought in a crew and cut a huge hole in the center of the main stage. They built a swimming pool for him. That's how we solve problems here: We throw money at them."

"Nice work if you can get it," Leah said.

Her attention was once more drawn to her computer, where another video window had just popped up. It showed a view from above the theater's back door. She blinked at the image.

It was Alex, unlocking the door.

"Look, I gotta go," Leah said suddenly. "Something's come up."

"Are you okay?" Gloria asked, her concern apparent in her tone.

"Yes, I'm fine," Leah said. "It's Alex. He just came into the theater and I need to talk to him. We had sort of a weird thing happen last night."

"Weird fun or weird weird?"

"Neither," Leah said, as she stood up. "He tried to kiss me and I freaked and it got sort of messy. I need to go straighten things out with him."

"Well, call me right away after and don't leave out any of the juicy details."

"Yeah, sure thing," Leah said, clearly distracted. "I'll talk to you later."

She hit the END button on her phone and slipped it into her

pocket as she headed out of her office. She started to quickly run through her head what she wanted to say to Alex and how she wanted to say it. She was so concerned with preparing her speech that she didn't recognize what she'd missed on the video image.

What she hadn't immediately noticed was that, for some unknown reason, Alex had been wearing his complete Dr. Einstein costume, including the wig and the mustache.

* * *

"Alex?"

Leah's voice echoed without response in the empty green room, and it did so again when she repeated her one-word question in the dressing room area. She moved to Alex's seat at the make-up table, where she noticed he had already shed the mustache and wig he'd been wearing when he'd come in. And why had he been wearing them…?

That question left her mind instantly when she turned and saw the Marlon Brando photo which Lucas had taped to his makeup mirror. This reminded her of the conversation from the previous night, where the young actor had looked so sheepish–guilty, actually–when the subject of how to send an anonymous text had come up.

She had meant to call Detective Albertson that morning to tell him about the encounter, but the previous eight hours had been swallowed up by the budget, and so that phone call–like the rest of her To-Do list–had been an unintended casualty of her day-long struggle with numbers.

Persuaded that Alex wasn't in the basement, she headed back to the stairway, thinking he might be up on the stage instead. Leah pulled out her phone as she climbed the stairs, quickly scrolling through her recent calls to find Detective Albertson's phone number. She'd had no luck finding it by the time she got to the top of the stairs; she'd scanned through a long list of numbers, but none of them looked familiar. She silently berated herself for not having added Detective Albertson to her contacts.

Rather than return to her office–where his business card *might* be, unless it was on her dining room table at home–she dialed 411 instead as she made her way into the auditorium. The lights were on in the large room, but the stage appeared to be empty.

When she heard the voice in her ear, Leah asked the operator for the number of the Western District for the St. Paul Police department. Moments later she heard the phone ringing.

"Alex?" she yelled while she waited for her call to be answered. "Are you in here?"

There was no answer from the stage, but there was from on the phone.

"St. Paul Police, Western District. How can I direct your call?"

"Detective Mark Albertson, please," Leah said, as she made her way down the main aisle toward the stage.

"One moment."

Leah climbed the steps to the platform, thinking Alex might be backstage for some reason. She headed toward the set's kitchen door, but before she could open it, there was a voice in her ear.

"I'm sorry, who are you trying to reach again?" It was the same woman who had taken her call, but her friendly attitude had been replaced by a more puzzled tone.

"Detective Mark Albertson," Leah repeated. "I believe he works in Homicide."

There were several seconds of digital silence on the other end of the phone, which were then followed by the sound of someone rapidly flipping through several sheets of paper.

"I'm sorry, there is no Detective Mark Albertson in the Western District," she said, still flipping through pages. "Or anywhere within the St. Paul Police Department for that matter. Are you sure about that name?"

"Yes, I am," Leah began, but just then the kitchen door swung open and the phone was ripped from her hand. She turned to see Dr. Einstein looking right back at her. He held the phone to his ear.

"Sorry, I think we must have the wrong number." He hit the end button on the phone and then looked at Leah.

The costume was definitely the one Alex wore for the play, or something very close. But the voice was nothing like his.

It was the voice of Detective Mark Albertson.

CHAPTER TWENTY-ONE

"Surprised?"

Detective Albertson offered this question without any warmth or humor in his voice.

"Yes, I suppose so," Leah said slowly. "Certainly confused, that's for sure."

"It's not all that puzzling, really," Albertson said as he stepped through the kitchen doorway onto the stage. Leah looked down to see he held a small revolver in his gloved hand. It was pointed at her. "At least, it won't be to the police."

"The police?" Leah repeated. "I thought *you* were the police."

"Yes, I know," he said, stepping further on stage while keeping the gun trained on her. "That was the idea."

"Impersonating a police officer is against the law," Leah said, trying to sound more in control than she currently felt.

He smiled at her observation. "Well, if I get caught, I think that might be the least of my problems." He looked around the empty auditorium.

"No, I don't think the police–the real police–will find it puzzling at all," he continued. "Without much effort, they'll discover that you and your friend–it's Alex, right?–you and your friend had a bit of an altercation last night in the parking lot."

Leah remembered Alex's awkward attempt at a kiss and her

surprised, emotional reaction, realizing it certainly had been witnessed by at least three of the actors. And, she remembered, also by a shadowy figure near the theater.

"Then they'll find the surveillance footage, showing Alex coming into the building," Albertson continued. "And the footage showing him leaving several minutes later. And, of course, they'll find your dead body here on the stage. Perhaps even in the same window seat where he stashed that critic he killed."

"Alex didn't kill Ronald Hatchet," Leah said, surprised at the fury in her voice.

"No, of course he didn't. And he didn't push that old battle-ax, Joan O'Malley, down the stairs. Or send you threatening texts. But the evidence–like the burner phone I just left in his makeup table–will tell a different story."

Leah looked at Albertson for a long moment and then, without even wondering if it was permissible in this situation, she sat down heavily on one of the dining room chairs.

"I have absolutely no idea what's going on," she said quietly.

"Lots of things are going on," Albertson said. "Except for this show. This particular show is not going on. Not anymore."

Leah slowly looked around the set and then up at him. Although the wig and mustache did a pretty good job of masking his face, his eyes burned down at her with a dark, frightening concentration.

"Why do you hate this show?"

"Oh, I don't. On the contrary, I love this show," he said. "I really do love this show. I just have little patience with people who don't share my love of it. Or who have the audacity to criticize one particularly stellar performer in its decidedly-mixed cast."

Leah mentally ran through all the cast members of *Arsenic and Old Lace*, trying to find any connection between that list and this crazed man who was leveling a pistol in her direction.

"She should have played Aunt Abby, that was clear from the beginning. A major oversight in casting," he continued. His eyes had a slightly glazed look as he spoke. "And if I have my way, she will play that role in this show."

Leah looked up at him, not believing what she was about to say. "Doris. Doris Peppers. Aunt Martha. You did all of this just so that she could play Aunt Abby?"

"She would be wonderful," he said thoughtfully.

"But then they would need to find a new Aunt Martha, which would be a pretty hard thing to accomplish at this point," Leah said, not sure if rational arguments had any real place in this conversation. "Maybe impossible."

"She can play both parts. She knows all the lines and she would be brilliant."

"Both parts?" Leah repeated. "At the same time? How would that work?"

"Split personality," he said, as if it were the simplest idea in the world. "Teddy thinks he's Teddy Roosevelt. So why can't his aunt think she's two people? Piece of cake and she'd be great."

Leah looked at him for a long moment. "So, you're not really Mark Albertson," she began.

He shook his head. "Just playing a part."

"And in reality you are …?"

"Mark," he said. "Mark Peppers. Son of Doris and Albert Peppers."

"Albert's son," Leah said, as some of the pieces began to come together in her mind. "Mark Albertson."

"Detective Mark Albertson," he corrected. "Homicide division."

Leah thought back to the few conversations she'd ever had with Doris Peppers. One particular comment the older woman had made suddenly stood out.

"Doris said she'd been dealing with a sick relative," Leah said. "I assumed she meant her husband, Albert. But she was talking about you, wasn't she?"

"Perhaps," he said. "I recently came home from a long stay. Somewhere else. We've had our problems in the past, my mother and I, it's true. But I'm better now," he added, his lips widening into an unnerving grin. "I'm all better now."

"So when your mother got a bad review, from that critic, you felt you had to do something…" Leah began.

"Absolutely. You don't take rude comments like the ones he made lying down," he said. "At least I don't."

"And then there was the praise he heaped on Joan O'Malley," Leah continued as she quickly scanned the stage. For a play so steeped in murder, the set offered precious few defensive weapons. For a quick moment, she wished they had done *Deathtrap* instead. Lots of weapons on stage for that one and that play offered none of the problems she was currently facing.

"Outrageous," he said, as if he were completing her thought. "That review was pornographic in its praise of that loathsome woman."

"So with Joan out of the way, you thought your mother was the logical choice to step into the role," Leah continued. She already understood all this, but she also needed some time–just a little time–to figure out how to get out of this situation.

"But then you had to go and volunteer," he said, his tone registering the disgust he felt.

"Volunteer is a strong word," she said, remembering back on how Gloria had basically railroaded her into accepting the role in front of the Board. "It was not my idea. Far from it."

She looked at the bottle of Elderberry wine on the sideboard. Although it didn't actually contain any poison, she knew the bottle itself did have a certain degree of heft to it. However, she didn't think she could get to it before he used his gun on her.

"And so you think the police–the real police–will make the assumption that Alex did this, even though he doesn't have any real motive?"

"I think I've left enough compelling evidence to lead them in that direction, yes," he said. He gestured with the gun for her to get up. "If you're going to sit, then at least sit on the window seat. Then I won't have to carry the body so far."

Leah stood up, slowly. His words about leaving evidence that would be held against Alex had triggered a thought, and not a very positive one.

In her conversation with Gloria on the phone just a few minutes before, hadn't she mentioned to her friend that she had just seen Alex coming into the building? Although she knew now she'd been mistaken, there was no way she could get that correction to Gloria. Unless she found a way to unarm her deranged stage companion.

Leah walked across the set toward the window seat, remembering she'd taken this same journey only a week before, while interviewing that annoying directing candidate. She ran the events of those seven days through her mind, trying to come up with something–anything–she could do that would change the outcome of this scene. Even if she couldn't save herself, she thought, at least she could keep poor Alex from being tossed under the bus.

She arrived at the window seat and turned to Mark Peppers, who was still aiming his gun at her. "So I suppose that also means there weren't any plainclothes men in the audience the other night?"

He shook his head, still smiling that unnerving grin. "Not a one."

"But the police are going to wonder about you. You talked to Gloria. To Betsy. Even Kanisha saw you."

"Why should they wonder? Detective Dietz was on the case originally. I'm sure he'll be back on this one. Why would they even think to mention another cop who'd been asking questions? They'll be too broken up over your untimely death," he said as he gestured with the gun that she should take a seat.

Leah sat. The box creaked, oh-so slightly from her weight. "You won't get away with this," she finally said. She was feeling the same way she did when she couldn't remember lines during a show. The words she needed just weren't there.

"I believe I've already gotten away with it," he said, taking a step closer. "Right now we're just tying up some loose ends."

She looked up at him. "You seemed like such a nice guy."

"Thanks. It was just a performance," he said. "Acting runs in my family, you know."

She could see him begin to squeeze the trigger and she instinctively closed her eyes. But instead of the crack of a gunshot, the next sound she heard was a derisive laugh.

"Holy crap, this is just terrible. I'm sorry to interrupt, but for heaven's sake stop. Just stop, you're doing such a bad job of killing her that you're actually killing me."

Leah opened her eyes and looked toward the sound. Mark Peppers turned, re-directing the pistol toward the set's kitchen door.

Dylan stood in the doorway, shaking his head in disgust.

"What the hell are you rehearsing here, *The Mousetrap*?" he said as he sauntered on-stage. The swinging door swung out and then in, hitting him on the backside and giving him a little boost into the set. He looked disheveled and hungover, like he'd just woken up after a long bender.

"Look, I don't want to step on any toes here," he continued as he moved toward them, "because I fully respect the sanctity of the rehearsal process. But someone has to pull the plug on this debacle right now."

Both Leah and Mark Peppers were about to speak, but Dylan was on a roll. He pointed to the young man holding the gun.

"Okay–the terrible text aside–first things first," Dylan said. "What is your intention in this scene? Everything is about intention and obstacle. What do you want and what is standing in your way of getting it? Because I'm getting nothing from you. Literally nothing."

"Dylan, this isn't a rehearsal," Leah began, but he cut her off.

"You've got that right. This is a train wreck."

"Who is this?" Mark Peppers asked as he stepped back, alternating the aim of his gun between the two other people on the stage.

"It's Dylan," Leah said. "We used to work together."

"We didn't just work together, we created together. And we created far better work than this. Really powerful stuff," Dylan said. "My god, Leah, you've gone from playing Mother Courage to playing Miss Marple? I can't see how you think this new gig is anything but a step down."

"Dylan, you don't understand," she began.

"You're right, I don't understand anything," he said as he stepped toward her, walking past Mark Peppers, ignoring the gun aimed at him. "Since you left, my mind has been a jumble. I'm lost. Simply lost. Come home with me." He gave her his best lost-puppy-dog look.

"This is my home now," she said, amazed to be having this conversation in the midst of being murdered.

"But we have history," he continued, apparently oblivious to the gun which was now focused squarely on his back. "Think of the roles we've played together and the magic we've created onstage. George and Martha. Petruchio and Kate. The Scottish King and his wife. We were like Lunt and Fontanne. And think of the roles we have yet to play…"

His words were cut off as Mark Peppers jabbed the gun sharply into the base of Dylan's spine.

"This is the last scene either one of you will be playing," he said as he gave Dylan a second jab with the nose of the pistol.

"Hey," Dylan said as he swung around. He looked at the gun and then up at the man holding it. ""What's the idea?"

"The idea is that the police will now find *two* bodies," Mark Peppers said as he stepped back to survey the pair. "Our friend, Alex, enraged with jealousy, kills Leah and her boyfriend, leaving their bloodied bodies strewn across the stage in a dramatic and homicidal tableau."

Dylan, genuinely confused, looked to Leah. "What's his deal?"

"He's the one who killed the critic. Tried to kill the actress. Threatened me," she explained quickly.

"I'm really out of the loop on this one," Dylan said. "What's going on?"

"Intention and obstacle," Leah explained, using terms she knew he'd understand. "His intention is that he wants to kill us.

For real. And sadly, right now, there are precious few obstacles in his path."

"As it should be," Mark Peppers agreed.

"And there's nothing we can do about it?" Dylan asked, looking to Leah for a solution.

"I'm afraid not," she said.

"There's really nothing we can do?" he repeated, the desperation rising audibly in his voice.

Something about Dylan repeating this question struck a chord in Leah. She remembered where she'd heard a similar exchange and hoped–desperately hoped–he would remember as well.

"Well, have you heard, but something hard of hearing?" she said, turning to him harshly. *"They call me Katharina that do talk of me."*

He looked at her, his face a sea of confusion, clearly not hearing his cue. "What?"

"They call me Katharina that do talk of me," she repeated, louder than the first time. For a long moment there was nothing. And then she saw a light go on behind his eyes. He shifted his body weight, taking on a more playful stance.

"You lie, in faith; for you are called plain Kate," he barked back at her.

Dylan's posture had entirely changed and he actually started to look larger and more imposing as he continued the speech. *"And bonny Kate and sometimes Kate the curst. Take this of me, Kate of my consolation; hearing thy mildness praised in every town, thy virtues spoke of, and thy beauty sounded, yet not so deeply as to thee belongs, myself am moved to woo thee for my wife."*

He began to move toward her. Leah backed away as she spoke.

"Moved! In good time," she said as Dylan approached her. She continued to back away, forcing Mark Peppers–who was now standing behind her–to back away as well. *"Let him that moved you hither remove you hence: I knew you at the first. You were a moveable."*

"Why, what's a moveable?" Dylan said, his face breaking into a wide grin.

"*A join'd stool*," Leah shot back. She continued to move away from him, moving backward.

"*Thou hast hit it*," Dylan said, closing the distance between them. "*Come, sit on me.*"

"*Asses are made to bear, and so are you.*"

"*Women are made to bear, and so are you.*"

"What the hell are you two doing?" Mark Peppers said, stumbling backward as the arguing couple stalked each other across the stage.

Dylan–seemingly oblivious–continued to advance on Leah. "*Come, come, you wasp,*" he said. "*In faith, you are too angry.*"

"*If I be waspish, best beware my sting,*" Leah said, skillfully putting one of the set's overstuffed chairs between herself and Dylan.

Mark Peppers swung his gun wildly from one to the other as the two actors maneuvered their way across the stage.

"*My remedy is then,*" Dylan said, pushing the chair aside with one quick shove, "*to pluck it out.*"

Leah grabbed another, smaller chair, holding it in front of her as she backed across the stage. "*Ay, if the fool could find it where it lies.*"

Dylan faked left and then pounced forward to the right. Leah anticipated both moves and dodged his outreached hand.

"*Who knows not where a wasp does wear his sting?*" Dylan said grinning at her skilled move. "*In his tail.*"

"*In his tongue,*" Leah shot back as she made a quick move around the couch. Mark Peppers matched her moves, scrambling backwards, nearly stumbling on the edge of the large, worn rug that was spread out by the couch.

"*Whose tongue?*" Dylan said.

"*Yours, if you talk of tails,*" she said, now a little out of breath. He made a playful grab at her. "*And so, farewell.*"

Leah made a wide arc with her arm and swung around, performing a text-book stage slap. She stepped backward and

Mark Peppers matched this move, taking his own quick step backward.

A look of surprise lit up his face as his feet found no stage beneath them. He dropped straight down, off the edge of the stage and then he sailed backward. He landed with a solid clunk against the front row of seats, slamming his head into an armrest. His gun dropped to the floor and his crumpled body followed a moment later.

"I swear I'll cuff you, if you strike again," Dylan said, but the acting went out of his voice about halfway through the sentence. He wandered over to Leah and they both looked down at the unconscious body slumped on the hard floor in front of the first row.

"Who is that guy again?" Dylan asked. Petruchio was now entirely gone and instead Dylan had reverted back into his natural dudeness.

"I really have no idea," Leah said as she pulled a strand of hair from across her face. "And I hate to admit it, but he's one heck of a good actor."

CHAPTER TWENTY-TWO

"If you have any brains, you'll hire a playwright and turn this story into the first show of the next season," Gloria said with a laugh. She waved at a passing waiter, gesturing that her wine glass had become, somehow, mysteriously empty.

"Oh, I don't think so. It strikes me as too unbelievable to be a play, and this is coming from someone who did forty performances of *The Star-Spangled Girl*," Leah said. She reached for another slice of the terrific bread, thought better of it and then reversed her decision. A moment later, she was slathering it with warm butter.

Her adventure with the murderous Mark Peppers was already two days behind her, but Leah's head was still spinning from that encounter and the events of the last ten days. Lunch in the swanky restaurant at Gloria's workplace was designed to help her debrief and refocus. And it was also a fine excuse for Gloria to have a couple glasses of wine in the middle of the day.

"So this guy gets out of the loony bin, discovers his mother got a bad review and decides his best course of action is to murder the critic and incapacitate the leading lady, so his mother can take over the role?" Gloria spit out this scenario so quickly that it took Leah a moment to take it all in.

"I think that's it, essentially," Leah said.

"And he also went so far as to actually pose as one of the investigating officers?" Gloria added with a shake of her head. "That's ballsy."

"It really was," Leah agreed.

Gloria leaned in. "And it didn't seem weird to you that you got interviewed by one police detective—"

"Detective Dietz," Leah said.

"And then yet another homicide detective stops by to interview you as well?"

Leah shrugged. "What do I know about murder investigations?"

"Of course, it didn't hurt that he was cute."

"I don't really think that was a factor," Leah said. "Although you're not wrong," she added with a sly smile.

"And you had no idea that you were working alongside this killer's mother the whole time?"

Leah shook her head. "No," she said. "And to be fair, Doris didn't have any idea either. Detective Dietz tells me she feels terrible about it."

"As one would," Gloria agreed.

"The thing is," Leah said, "I could have figured the whole thing out right away if I'd only taken the time to glance over at the photos Doris had pinned up by her make-up mirror."

"She'd hung up a family portrait of some kind, did she, showing her son in a straight-jacket?"

"No, but she did have a photo of her late husband, Al."

"Albert," Gloria corrected. "And his son?"

"Absolutely. A photo of Detective Mark Albertson, big as life," Leah said. "I just never bothered to look." She shook her head and grabbed another piece of bread. The butter was gone, so she dipped it into a small dish of olive oil.

"And who would have ever pegged Dylan as the guy who'd waltz in and save the day?" Gloria said as she neatly swapped her empty wine glass for a new, full one offered by the waiter.

"'Save the day' might be laying it on a bit thick," Leah said. "However, you can't beat his timing."

"So he'd been hiding in the theater for days?"

Leah nodded. "That's what he told me. He had nowhere to stay, so he hid in the men's room during the second act of the show, and then went down to the green room and lifted a key from one of the actors during the curtain call."

"Because he knew no one would be down there during the curtain call," Gloria said.

"Exactly. He'd been sleeping in furniture storage ever since. And of course he's been dining out on our prop food from the show."

"Clever boy," Gloria said. "How did he avoid the surveillance system once that was in place?"

Leah smiled. "He came in and out through the overhead garage door in the scene shop," she said. "It locks from the inside, so we didn't bother putting a camera back there. But he saw them installing the cameras over the front and back doors, so he just left the overhead door unlocked and came and went as he pleased."

"So much for the theater's airtight security system," Gloria said as she took a long sip from her wine.

"You get what you pay for," Leah said, remembering the lengthy bid process she'd had to go through to secure a vendor. "Had we used the Qualification-Based Selection process I recommended, we might have gotten a better system and still paid less."

"Try telling that to the Board," Gloria snorted. "Wait, I just remembered–you did! I still recall how Claudia Moffatt just kept saying over and over, 'We always go with the low bid, we always go with the low bid.' What a crazy lush she is."

Gloria took another long sip of her wine and Leah decided not to mention the irony inherent in her friend's statement. Instead, she thought about Claudia Moffatt and made a mental note to call and check in on her as soon as she got back to the theater.

"So at least now things can get back to normal," Gloria

continued as the waiter returned and placed the bill discretely on the table, midway between the two women.

"I'm not sure I've experienced 'normal' yet at the Como Lake Players," Leah said as she reached for her purse and began to dig into it in search of her credit card.

Gloria held up a firm hand. "This one's on me," she said. "Or, actually, on the theater."

"Which theater?" Leah asked. "Because the one I work for can't afford lavish expense account lunches."

"Well luckily, the one I work for can," Gloria said as she slapped her black plastic card on top of the bill with a little more force than might have been necessary.

* * *

Leah was relieved that she had opted out of the wine offered to her at lunch. Gloria only had to make it as far as the elevator, which would take her to her fifth floor office. Leah's post-lunch activities included driving the five miles from the well-funded theater complex on the river to the ragged old church which housed her financially-challenged community theater.

She had just parked her car in the rutted parking lot and was headed toward the theater's back door when a voice called out to her.

"Leah!"

She turned to see Dylan, who was in the midst of tossing an old gym bag into the trunk of his even older Ford Fiesta. He was still dressed in the worn jeans and sweatshirt he'd been wearing when he appeared on-stage in the midst of her confrontation with Mark Peppers. Despite his liberal use of the theater's sleeping and eating accommodations, Dylan had apparently opted against using the washer and dryer in the costume shop.

"I'm glad I caught you," he continued as he slammed the trunk's lid. Even from this distance, Leah could see the dust that action raised on the old car; it might have even loosened some small chunks of rust as well. "I'm just about to head out."

"To the Bakersfield Playhouse?" Leah said as she changed her course and headed toward him.

"That's right," he said with a laugh. "Those spears aren't going to carry themselves."

"I'm sure your parts will be more significant than spear carrier," Leah said. She was surprised that her feelings of annoyance at Dylan had entirely subsided and had been replaced with something else. What was it? Tolerance? Affection, maybe?

"Well, whatever," Dylan said, waving it off. "I'm just happy to get the work."

They stood an awkward distance apart, each unsure of the true mood of this encounter.

"Anyway," he continued. "I'm glad I caught you. Before I left."

"Me too," she said. "I just finished a long lunch with Gloria."

"Ah, Gloria," he said with a grin. "She really hates me. What was her blood alcohol level at the end of the meal?"

"She doesn't hate you," Leah countered. "But, yeah, she was pretty sloshed by the time the check came."

Another awkward moment.

"Well, have a safe trip. And let me know where you land," she said as she stepped forward and gave him a quick hug. He returned the short hug and then stepped back and looked down at her.

"I'm sorry about…" he began, but his voice trailed off. "I guess I'm sorry about everything."

"It's okay," she said. "As it turns out, when I really needed you, you were right there."

"That's my gift," he said as he flashed his million-dollar grin. "The white knight, riding in at the last second to save the damsel in distress."

"Maybe next time, don't wait until literally the last second."

"Understood," he said. He opened the car's driver door and was about to climb into the ancient vehicle, but then turned back. Before she could react, he gave her a quick kiss on the forehead. Then he was in the car and had started the engine.

Moments later, he roared out of the parking lot, raising a cloud of dust as the car bumped its way toward the street.

Leah watched him go for a few moments longer than might have been necessary, then spun around and continued toward the theater.

* * *

"Do you have time for one quick thing?" Betsy had stuck her head into Leah's office, peering at her from around the door jamb.

Leah looked up from her computer. She had just about tamed the new budget, but was searching the seemingly endless Excel document to ensure she hadn't duplicated any line entries. She was still hoping to find a spare $1,500 to repair at least a few of the more egregious potholes in the parking lot and was having trouble finding anything close to that amount.

Leah glanced at the clock in the corner of her screen. "I've got a few minutes before the speed-through," she said. Her budgeting had already been interrupted on the screen several times as the security system popped on to inform her that various actors were making their way into the building. She clicked SAVE and closed the spreadsheet. "What's up?"

"You've got to interview one more candidate for the directing slot," Betsy said.

"There's one more?" Leah said. She thought back through the meager list of candidates, pretty sure she had spoken to all of them at least once.

"A late entry," Betsy explained.

"Oh, okay," Leah said. Although annoyed at the surprise nature of this interview, she was glad to be given the option of talking to one more contender. She hadn't been overly impressed with the folks she had met so far.

"He's waiting for you in the Board room," Betsy added before disappearing around the corner to her office.

Leah made the short trip between her office and the conference room. The moment she walked in, she immediately recognized its only other occupant, even though he was across the room and had his back to her. He was studying a large banner which ran across the length of the room. On it was listed every show the theater had produced in its long history.

"You?" she exclaimed, her voice coming out louder than she had intended. "You're the directing candidate?"

Alex turned from studying the shows listed on the banner. "So this theater has only done *The Importance of Being Earnest* twice over the years? That seems low," he said, turning back to doublecheck his assessment. "I mean, it is a staple of the traditional community theater."

"You're the directing candidate?" Leah repeated.

Alex looked around the room to see who she might be talking to. "Me?" he said, incredulous. "Don't be crazy. I can't direct traffic."

"Betsy said there was a directing candidate in the Board room," Leah said. She considered heading over to Betsy's office to clear up the mystery, but Alex's voice stopped her.

"There is," he said quickly as he moved across the room toward her. "You see, I was chatting with some people around here and they were saying you were having trouble finding someone to direct that show. *The Importance of Being Earnest*. And it occurred to me, I know the perfect person."

"Who?" Leah asked. It felt like the long lunch followed by hours spent in front of the budget spreadsheet had turned her brain to mush.

"You," Alex said. And then he pointed at her to help drive the point home.

"Me?" Leah said. "Why me?"

"Simple. You understand comedy, you understand how to work with actors," he began. "And face it, you're going to be in the building anyway, so you might as well direct the darned thing."

Leah started to speak, but then she stopped and considered his argument. Back in New York, Dylan had always insisted on being the director of any of the shows they had worked on, even though he often stole liberally from the smart suggestions she made throughout the process from the sidelines.

"I should direct it," she said. The short sentence started out as a question but landed as a solid statement by the time she had reached the end of it. She said it again, just to emphasize the point. "I should direct it."

"Glad you agree," Alex said.

"And you have to be in it," Leah said, as she began to cast the show in her mind. "As Algernon."

"Or the other one," he offered. He glanced down at his watch. "We can talk about that later, we have a speed-through to get to," he said as he moved toward the door.

"Of course, the downside is that I can't be in it then," Leah said as she followed him out of the room.

"That's too bad, because that's a good part for you at this age," Alex said.

"Cecily?" Leah said.

"No, not that one."

"Gwendolyn?"

Alex shook his head. "No, I think you're more the Lady Bracknell type, don't you?" he said.

"What?"

"Well, she has the best speeches," he continued. "And, let's face it, you have proven your particular skill at playing dowagers and women of, shall we say, a certain age."

She raised a hand toward him, staring him down. There was a moment of tense silence between them.

"Plus, you'd spend far less time in the make-up chair than you would if you played Cecily or Gwendolyn." He smiled at her and winked.

Her hand came down, missing him by inches, and he took off down the stairs, with Leah in quick pursuit.

GRAB THE NEXT BOOK IN THE SERIES!

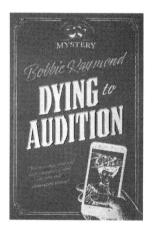

DYING TO AUDITION
A Como Lake Players Mystery (#2)
"This new cozy series will keep you guessing until the very end." – *StoreyBook Reviews*

One actor gave a killer audition. The only question is, will they kill again?

What begins as a simple evening of auditions for *The Importance of Being Earnest* turns into a deadly mystery for Leah and her cast.

First one actor is murdered, then another disappears, leaving Leah in the dangerous position of trying to solve the crimes while re-casting her show.

Will she make it to Opening Night before one more tragedy strikes her comedy?

OTHER BOOKS FROM ALBERT'S BRIDGE BOOKS

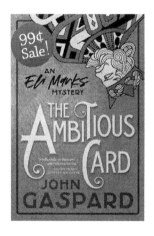

THE AMBITIOUS CARD
An Eli Marks Mystery (#1)
The life of a magician isn't all kiddie shows and card tricks. Sometimes it's murder. Especially when magician Eli Marks very publicly debunks a famed psychic, and said psychic ends up dead. The evidence, including a bloody King of Diamonds playing card (one from Eli's own Ambitious Card routine), directs the police right to Eli.

As more psychics are slain, and more King cards rise to the top, Eli can't escape suspicion. Things get really complicated when romance blooms with a beautiful psychic, and Eli discovers she's the next target for murder, and he's scheduled to die with her. Now Eli must use every trick he knows to keep them both alive and reveal the true killer.

Available in eBook, Paperback, Audiobook and Hardcover editions.

OTHER BOOKS FROM ALBERT'S BRIDGE BOOKS

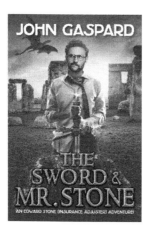

"The Sword & Mr. Stone."

A Wild Modern-Day Quest for King Arthur's Magical Sword, Excalibur!

Insurance adjuster Edward Stone's quiet life is completely upset when he's drawn into a wild search for King Arthur's fabled lost sword, Excalibur.

From the towering monuments of Stonehenge to the dark mists of Loch Ness, Stone finds himself battling evil forces intent upon possessing this long-lost treasure.

It's only when he embraces the magical nature of the legend that's Stone is finally able to harness the epic forces behind Excalibur, the Sword of Power.

"A hero is no braver than an ordinary man, but he is brave five minutes longer." — Ralph Waldo Emerson

Grab this funny, gripping adventure today! Available in eBook, Paperback and Hardcover editions.

OTHER BOOKS FROM ALBERT'S BRIDGE BOOKS

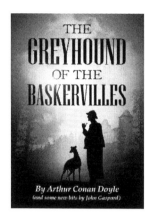

THE GREYHOUND OF THE BASKERVILLES

This is new edition of Arthur Conan Doyle's classic mystery, "The Hound of the Baskervilles." It's the same story.

Mostly. That is, it contains the same characters, the same action, and much of the same dialogue. What's different?

Well, it's a little shorter, a little leaner, a little less verbose in some sections.

But the chief difference is that it's now narrated by a dog. A greyhound, in fact, named Septimus.

In this new edition, he tells his story of how he became "The Greyhound of the Baskervilles." Same story, new tail.

Available in eBook, Paperback, Audiobook and Hardcover editions.

OTHER BOOKS FROM ALBERT'S BRIDGE BOOKS

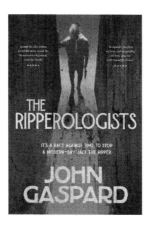

THE RIPPEROLOGISTS

The Ripperologists is a contemporary thriller about two competing experts who are forced to work together to beat the clock when a copycat serial killer begins recreating Jack the Ripper's 1888 murder spree.

Set against the backdrop of the fascinating subculture of Ripperologists, the story takes equal stabs at the disparate worlds of publishing, Ripper studies, fan conventions, and Internet chatrooms, as our two unlikely heroes employ their (often contrary) knowledge of a 120-year-old phantom to hunt down a modern killer.

Available in eBook, Paperback, Audiobook and Hardcover editions.

ABOUT THE AUTHOR

John Gaspard writes the *Como Lake Players* mystery series, under the pen name Bobbie Raymond.

John is author of the Eli Marks mystery series as well as three other stand-alone novels, *"The Sword & Mr. Stone," "The Greyhound of the Baskervilles," "A Christmas Carl,"* and *"The Ripperologists."*

In real life, John's not a magician, but he has directed six low-budget features that cost very little and made even less - that's no small trick.

He's also written multiple books on the subject of low-budget filmmaking. Ironically, they've made more than the films. Those books (*"Fast, Cheap and Under Control"* and *"Fast, Cheap and Written That Way"*) are available in eBook, Paperback and audiobook formats.

John lives in Minnesota and shares his home with his lovely wife, several dogs, a few cats and a handful of pet allergies.

Find out more at: https://www.albertsbridgebooks.com

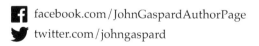

facebook.com/JohnGaspardAuthorPage
twitter.com/johngaspard

Manufactured by Amazon.ca
Bolton, ON